AND THEN MINE ENEMY

ALISON STUART

And Then Mine Enemy

Copyright © 2016 by Alison Stuart

ISBN: 9780995434233

This edition: Oportet Publishing 2018

Editor: Annie Seaton

Cover Design: Fiona Jayde

Formatting: Ebony McKenna

This is a work of fiction. Names, characters, places, brands, media, and incidents are either the product of the author's imagination or are used fictitiously. The author acknowledges the trademarked status and trademark owners of various products referenced in this work of fiction, which have been used without permission. The publication/use of these trademarks is not authorised, associated with, or sponsored by the trademark owners.

Discover other titles by Alison Stuart at www.alisonstuart.com

AND THEN MINE

ENEMY

A romantic saga of the English Civil War

BOOK ONE of FEATHERS IN THE WIND

ALISON STUART

And Then Mine Enemy

A family ripped apart in a country divided by war...

England 1642: Hardened mercenary, Adam Coulter returns to England sickened by violence, seeking only peace, but he finds England on the brink of civil war. He has seen first-hand what that will mean for every man, woman and child and wants no part of it.

King or Parliament? Neutrality is not an option and Adam can only be true to his conscience, not the dictates of his family.

Having escaped a loveless marriage, Perdita Gray has found much needed sanctuary and the love of a good man, but her fragile world begins to crumble as Adam Coulter bursts into her life. This stranger brings not only the reality of war to her doorstep but reignites an old family feud, threatening everything and everyone she holds dear.

As the war and family tensions collide around them, Adam and Perdita are torn between old loyalties and a growing attraction that must be resisted.

'I am a feather for each wind that blows.'
- William Shakespeare, *The Winter's Tale*, 2.3

Chapter One

ENGLAND JULY 1642

A shudder of rain slewed across the sodden countryside, sending its cold fingers cutting through Adam's already saturated cloak. He huffed out a misty breath and straightened his aching shoulders. Not for the first time he cursed his brother for summoning him to a meeting Adam knew would inevitably end in grief and recrimination.

The remote inn loomed out of the gloaming and led on by the cheerful light spilling through the front windows, Adam urged his weary horse forward. The miserable beast, the mud dragging at its every step, plodded on.

A young boy ran from the stable, a sack over his head and shoulders. Adam threw him the reins and taking a deep breath, strode into the inn. He tossed his hat and gloves to the innkeeper, his numbed fingers fumbled at the ties of his cloak.

'His Lordship's in the private parlour.' The innkeeper scowled as he held the dripping garb at arm's length.

Adam pushed open the door the man indicated. The two men seated beside a cheerful fire burning in the wide hearth, rose to their feet. His half-brothers schooled their faces to a neutrality that Adam knew would not last. As they faced him across the room, a growing sense of despondency gripped him. Once more the cuckoo in the nest, always the acknowledged baseborn son but not even given the protection of his father's name.

Denzil Marchant, just as Adam remembered him, tall and powerful, with a mane of tawny hair like his father, and his younger brother Robin, as tall but of a slighter, elegant build, his hair more auburn and sleekly curling.

'Denzil, Robin,' Adam acknowledged them as he stepped into the room. 'I wish I could say, well met, but I would be lying.'

'Adam Coulter.' The deliberate use of his full name jarred, as Denzil no doubt intended. 'I would scarcely have recognised you. Hardly the darling of the court now, are you?'

'I found lovelocks and pearl earrings something of a hindrance to the life of a soldier.' Without waiting to be invited, Adam poured himself a full measure from the bottle of wine that stood on the table, hoping that they would not mark that his hand shook.

'Foul weather,' he remarked, raising his cup. 'Is there space beside the fire for me?'

Denzil stood aside and Adam took his place beside the fire. Water dripped on to the hearthstone and steam rose from his damp clothing.

Adam took a mouthful of wine. It was surprisingly good for such an isolated inn.

'How is your beautiful wife, Denzil?' Even after all these years he could not hide the note of derision in his voice.

Denzil's already high colour deepened and his brows drew together at the mention of Louise. 'Louise is with the queen in France.'

So, that particular wound still bled, Adam thought.

'So much has happened in the last years, Denzil. I believe I should now call you Lord Marchant. When did Father die?'

'Some eighteen months past. Even on his deathbed he refused to call you his son,' Denzil responded with narrowed eyes as he watched the barb go home.

As intended, the cruel words cut like a sword thrust to Adam's heart.

'Why did you come back to England?' Robin spoke for the first time, his tone light and conciliatory.

Adam turned his attention to his youngest brother. How old would Robin be now, twenty-one, twenty-two?

'Because I'm tired of fighting other people's wars and thought I should come home and find a peaceful occupation. Instead I have returned to a country that talks of war as if it is an inevitability.' Adam turned back to look at Denzil from over the top of his wine cup. 'Is this why you sent for me?'

'I had heard you'd returned and we have need of men like you, Coulter,' Denzil said.

'What do you mean, men like me?' Adam set the empty wine cup down on a nearby table and turned to face the fire, casually rearranging the smouldering logs with a poker.

'Hardened soldiers. Men who know what they're doing. England is about to go to war led by a bunch of country squires whose only idea of warfare is what they have read in a book.'

Adam glanced at him. 'Men like you, Denzil?'

His brother's moustache twitched and his eyes narrowed.

'Tell me what has happened to England in the six years I have been away? What have I come back to? Because it is not the country I left.'

Denzil's brow furrowed. 'It is indeed a sad country where a King cannot govern without being hindered at every turn by the machinations of his so-called Parliament.'

'It seems to me,' Adam straightened. and kept his voice low and even, 'that we have a King who believes he can rule contrary to the will of the people.'

'The king's greatest enemy is his own parliament,' Robin said.

'The king's greatest enemy is himself.' Adam turned his gaze on Robin.

'What do you mean?' Robin came around to stand beside Denzil.

'I served the king, Robin. I know the character of the man. He has a firm and unshakable belief in what he sees as his divine right to rule. Parliament may have forced him to hand over his powers of taxation and his courts but I cannot see him ever agreeing to surrender his right to choose his own counsellors or to control his army. Nor will he agree to abolish the bishops and the Prayer Book. Isn't that what parliament has asked of him?'

The colour rose higher in Denzil's florid cheeks. 'All that and more, Coulter. They are saying that the king can no longer be trusted to make his own judgments about the men best able to advise him or to control his army. They have driven him from London.'

Adam thrust away from the fireplace and paced the room, running his hand through his hair. 'God's death, do these people who talk of war have any idea what damage a civil war can wreak? I've seen civil war at first hand and I've no wish to see the likes of it in this country.' He turned to face Denzil. 'Whatever you want of me, Denzil, I'll have no part of it. I've come home with enough in my purse for a small estate and I intend to turn my hand to the till, not the sword.'

Denzil snorted. 'You'll be bored of that within a month, or you're not the man I remember. Coulter.' His tone softened, almost wheedling. 'Let's put the past behind us. You were young. I can forgive you your indiscretion.'

Indiscretion? Was that the price of a man's life?

Adam's shoulders tensed in the old, familiar way. 'What do you want of me, Denzil?'

'I'm offering you a commission in my regiment of horse.'

Adam raised an eyebrow. 'You have a regiment of horse?'

Denzil raised his chin. 'I've raised the militia.'

'Before the king has even raised his standard? No thank you. I want no part of this accursed affair.'

'Is that your final answer, Coulter?'

'It is. I would be pleased to do as you ask and put the past behind us, but I cannot in all conscience join this venture at your side.'

Denzil's jaw tightened and Adam braced himself for an explosion. Instead his brother threw up his hands and sighed. 'What will you do?'

'I will do as I said. Continue my journey to Shropshire where I intend to inspect a property and God willing, that is where I shall stay.'

Denzil glanced at Robin. 'You think Shropshire far enough away to escape our troubles?'

'No. I have lived through civil war, Denzil. It is insidious. It will seek out even the most remote corners of this poor, benighted country.'

Robin cleared his throat. 'We have been wondering about Aunt Joan.'

This shift in the conversation took Adam by surprise. 'Aunt Joan?'

'Yes. She was recently widowed,' Robin looked up at Denzil. 'Denzil?'

'I am now head of this family and I am naturally concerned for her welfare in the coming conflict.'

'That's very touching, but like myself Joan has hardly been your concern since her marriage.' Adam could hear the sarcasm in his voice.

Denzil's jaw tightened again and he blew out a breath. 'What Robin is trying to say is I am prepared to put her enmity with father aside and offer her the protection of her former home at Marchants, should she wish it.'

Adam laughed. 'Why in God's sweet name would she want to go to Marchants? She hated the place as much as I did.'

'Damn it, Coulter.' Denzil brought a powerful fist down on the table. 'You are trying my patience. As head of the family I believe it my place to try and heal the wounds that have divided us for too long. If you are passing Preswood, can you at least take her my message.'

Adam paused. 'Preswood is near Stratford from memory and it would be good to see her again. Very well, I will take her your message.' At the door, Adam turned to face his brothers. 'I suppose I should thank you for the olive branch Denzil, but it's too late. We were a family divided long before this became a country divided.' He inclined his head and walked out of the room, resisting the temptation to slam the door behind him.

Chapter Two

Perdita pushed the food around her plate with the knife, conscious that through the interminable meal, Simon's gaze had not moved from her. Across from her, Elizabeth nattered about some matter of local gossip that required no more than the occasional grunt or tsk in response. As Joan's gaze flickered from Perdita to Simon and back again, her brow creased.

'Forgive me,' Joan said. 'Perdita? Simon? Have you quarrelled?'

Simon's eyes widened. 'Quarrelled?' He glanced at Perdita. 'Far from it.' He rose to his feet, his glass in hand, and looked around the table. His gaze returned to Perdita and he smiled, a smile of such sweetness and love that her heart skipped a beat. Was it too late to renege? To turn back the clock to the sweet friendship she had treasured with this man?

'Joan, Elizabeth.' Simon addressed his stepmother and sister. 'It may come as something of a surprise, but Perdita, our dearest kinswoman, has consented to be my wife.'

A squeal of delight ensued from Elizabeth. Joan, not given to overt displays of emotion, cast a quick scrutinising glance in Perdita's direction and she looked away.

'I'm delighted,' Joan said and raised her glass. 'I wish you both much happiness in the years ahead. Were your father still alive, Simon, I know he would approve.'

Elizabeth beamed at Perdita from across the table. 'How I have always longed for a sister.'

Perdita knew she should say something. Her fingers twisted in the chain of her mother's locket as she struggled to find adequate words to cover the tumult of emotions raging in her mind. Simon had resumed his seat but he still gazed at her, a huge grin on his cheerful, freckled face. He leaned across the table, grasping her left hand in his square dependable fingers, pressing it to his lips. He did not need to speak - Simon was incapable of dissembling in either word or gesture.

Perdita pushed back her pangs of guilt. She did not deserve such adoration, not when she felt incapable of returning those feelings. When Simon had first asked, she had hesitated a long while, but he had been patient and his very patience had worn down her resistance. Finally she had given him the answer he sought, telling herself that Simon was a dear person, comfortable and dependable, and compared with the endless years of lonely widowhood that stretched ahead of her or the prospect of another forced marriage to the likes of Samuel Gray, she could certainly do much worse. Besides their kinship was distant, Her grandmother and Simon's grandmother had been distantly related but no closer relationship existed.

She may not have loved Simon in the romantic sense of the word, but she liked him, loved him as a friend, and perhaps friendship would be enough. Love could come later.

She smiled and squeezed his hand.

'Have you thought about when the wedding is to take place?' Elizabeth asked.

Simon released Perdita's hand and straightened in his chair. 'I confess, I've not given that much thought. With the present state of affairs, it may be prudent to wait until closer to Christmas.'

'What do you mean?' Elizabeth asked.

'You know what I mean, Bess.' Simon said impatiently. 'War is coming.'

'Oh, not that again.' Bess dismissed the troubles between the king and his parliament with a wave of her hand. 'I'm so bored with that.'

'Bess,' Simon began but the crash of a door and the sound of raised voices stopped him mid remonstrance, 'confound it. What is that racket?'

Ludovic, the Clifford's steward, a large, laconic man of foreign background who had been attached to Geoffrey Clifford from long before his marriage to Joan, appeared at the door.

'There is a gentleman here, who insists on an audience with Mistress Clifford,' he said but got no further as a tall man with rough-cut dark brown hair strode into the room.

He swept the startled company a bow. 'Forgive my intrusion,' he said, rising to address them.

Joan set her glass down and rose slowly to her feet. 'Surely not? Adam?'

'Aunt Joan.' A broad grin split his tanned face and in two strides he had crossed to her, sweeping her off her feet into an embrace.

Bess cast her brother a quizzical glance.

'Good Lord.' Simon blasphemed, rising from his chair. 'Adam Coulter?'

'Simon Clifford.' Adam set his aunt back on the ground and seized Simon's hand. 'It's been a long time.' He looked at Joan and frowned. 'Your wedding, Aunt, if my memory serves me correctly?'

'Yes indeed. Ten years at least.' Joan, her face unusually flushed, recollected herself. 'Ludovic,' she ordered the steward. 'Set another place at the table. This is my nephew, Adam Coulter, who has been abroad these many years. A very welcome guest in this house.'

As Ludovic bowed and withdrew, Joan looked up at her nephew and tapped him on his chest. 'Why did you not send word for me to expect you?'

He flashed her a smile. 'I thought I might surprise you.'

Joan's hand flew to her throat. Perdita had never seen Joan so discomposed. 'Surprise me? Good heavens, Adam, you have just about killed me.' She looked around the table. 'Now, you are acquainted with Simon but I doubt you remember his sister, my stepdaughter, Elizabeth? She would have been barely twelve at our wedding.'

Bess had been staring open-mouthed at the stranger. She managed a wobbly curtsey and a gracious inclination of her head.

'Mistress Clifford, your servant,' Adam Coulter acknowledged.

His gaze moved to Perdita. 'And the last but not the least member of my household is our kinswoman, Perdita Gray.'

Coulter inclined his head. 'Mistress Gray.'

Perdita met the startling intensity of his light grey eyes with equanimity. 'Master Coulter, you are welcome to Preswood.'

Joan had never spoken of her family with Perdita, although Bess had told her the estrangement with the Marchants went back long before Joan's marriage to Geoffrey Clifford. Joan called him this man her nephew but why was he introduced as Adam Coulter, not Marchant?

Joan asked the question that burned on Perdita's lips. 'What brings you here, Adam?'

As he took his seat, Adam Coulter turned to his aunt. 'Denzil told me you have been recently widowed.'

The joy drained from Joan's face, the pain of her recent loss stark in her eyes. She raised a trembling hand to her mouth.

Perdita answered for her. 'Last winter,' she said. 'Lung fever.'

Perdita cast a glance around the table. The mention of Geoffrey Clifford brought back unhappy memories from them all. Bess bit her lip and pleated the material of her sleeve while Simon looked up at the ceiling.

Adam laid his hand over Joan's. 'I'm sorry, Joan. He was a good man.' His gaze swept the table. 'My condolences to all of you.'

Joan hefted a heavy sigh and squared her shoulders. 'We miss him, but Adam, did you say Denzil told you? When did you see him?'

Adam's mouth tightened in a grim, humourless smile. 'Somehow Denzil had word I had returned to London, probably through that irritating lawyer. He sent for me and like a good brother I went. The reunion was not a great success.'

Joan's lips parted but Simon interrupted. 'Last I heard you were abroad, Coulter, fighting the German wars. What brings you back to England?'

Perdita detected a momentary hesitation before Adam Coulter replied. 'Tired of the wandering life, Clifford. I've an eye to a small estate in the border country. In fact, I'm on my way there and promised Denzil I would deliver a message to Joan.'

Joan's lips twisted in a wry smile. 'A message for me? Is Denzil trying to mend the bridges his dear father burned. First you, and now me? Whatever next? What is his message?'

'In view of your recent widowhood, he is offering you a home at Marchants.'

Joan frowned. 'But I have a home here. Why would I want to return to Marchants?'

'He believes this country is coming to war and is concerned for your safety. Is that what you think, Clifford?'

War. That seemed to be all men could talk of these days. Perdita and Bess exchanged resigned glances. There had too many dinners recently that had descended into talk of war with the women banished to the parlour.

Simon shifted in his chair and he cleared his throat with a

quick sideways glance at Perdita. He knew her views on the subject. She tightened her lips as Simon said, 'I believe so. I already have orders from Lord Northampton to raise my militia in the king's name.'

Adam sighed. 'Then let us pray that wiser heads take counsel and stop this thing before it becomes too late.'

The look of resignation on his face belied his word and Perdita challenged him. 'You don't believe that, do you?'

He looked at her and shook his head. 'No. I think it's already too late. I've just passed through Stratford. Lord Brooke...?' He glanced at Simon for confirmation of the name, who nodded affirmation. 'Lord Brooke had called a muster of the Warwickshire Militia.'

'I know,' Simon said. 'A muster of those militia willing to take up the parliament' cause.'

Adam regarded Simon thoughtfully for a moment. 'I listened to what he had to say. He's an impressive man, Brooke. He talks sense.'

'He's a puritan with his own reasons for wanting parliament to prevail.' Simon paused. 'How many do you think he has gathered to his cause?'

Adam shrugged. 'Not as many as I'm sure he would have liked. A couple of hundred, no more, for all that he was offering the comers five shillings and plying them with food and drink.'

Simon nodded and smiled. 'That'll please Northampton. He's planning a muster at Stratford within the month for the king's cause. Naturally I will be attending.'

Perdita looked from one to the other. 'Are you saying that this must come to a choice? King or Parliament? Neighbour against neighbour?' Neither man replied but their silence gave her the answer. 'You men are making this thing a reality. The more you talk of it, the more it becomes a certainty,' she said.

Adam Coulter regarded her for a long moment. 'You are right,

Mistress Gray. England has talked itself into war and I fear it is too late to turn back.'

Simon coughed. 'Coulter, you're most welcome at Preswood. Indeed, if you have some days to spare, I have need of help with my men.' He smiled ruefully. 'I'm not much of a military hand. I've books of course, but it is not the same as practical experience.'

Adam turned to look at Simon. 'Don't ask me to take your side, Clifford. I've already told my brother that I've no wish to fight a civil war in my own country.'

'I'm not asking you to join me, Coulter, but I've a reluctant tenantry armed with antique weapons or whatever they can lay their hands on, and an order from Lord Northampton to present them properly trained at the muster. To be honest, I could use the help of an experienced soldier such as yourself.'

Adam glanced at his aunt. She leaned over and laid her hand on his. 'Stay a little while, Adam.'

He nodded. 'Very well, I'll give you a week, Clifford. What little help I can render is yours.'

A week? Perdita glanced at Simon, knowing his struggles to bring the tenants into some sort of order. From farmers to soldiers. Little wonder they were reluctant.

'Enough of politics,' Joan said. 'I am determined not to let this meal be spoiled by talk of things that, God willing, may never come to pass. This meal is a celebration, Adam. Let us raise our glasses to Simon and Perdita whose betrothal we are celebrating.'

Perdita glanced away as Adam Coulter's direct gaze fell on her again.

'Betrothed? And I have come like a beggar at the feast,' he said. 'I apologise for interrupting what should have been a happy meal with such dark talk.'

Perdita raised her eyes to meet his. 'I think, Master Coulter,' she said, 'that it is better that these things are talked of openly, for all our futures hang on these machinations.'

Joan clapped her hands. 'Enough, Perdita. My nephew has returned from the dead. Adam, I can't believe the change in you. Is this what soldiering abroad does for you? Do you remember Adam at my wedding, Simon? Lovelocks and a pearl earring, quite the courtier.'

Adam touched his left ear, where the faint indentation still marked a young man's fancy.

'That was a long time ago,' he said with a rueful smile, running a hand through his dark, rough-cut locks, bleached at the ends by long days in the sun.

'Over six years, Adam. Not a word,' his aunt chided.

'I never was a letter writer, aunt, and unfortunately for me, I spent a couple of those years immured in Leipzig Castle for my part at the battle of Vlotho.'

Joan gasped. 'I had no idea you were a prisoner. Was there a ransom set for your release? Isn't that how these things are arranged. If I had known...'

'My dear brother declined the ransom,' Adam said with a bitter smile twisting the corners of his mouth. He let out a breath and glancing around the table, he said, 'As you say, enough talk of dark memories.' He raised his glass. 'To Simon Clifford and his betrothed, and, God willing, to common sense and an end of this talk of war.'

Chapter Three

The three women sat in the window of the room the family called the great parlour, working on the banner Joan had designed for Simon's newly formed company of foot soldiers. Perdita found it a grim task. Every stitch seemed to draw the inevitability of war closer.

She looked up from her work and eased her cramped fingers, her gaze straying beyond the window to where Simon's motley contingent of reluctant tenantry drilled with ancient pikes. Their general air of gloom and despondency was not helped by the persistent heavy rain that weighed down their shapeless felt hats and soaked their new, blue uniform jackets.

Bess set down her end of the banner and sucked her finger. 'My needle is blunt,' she complained. 'Why do we have to use such heavy material?'

Perdita gave her kinswoman a withering glance. 'Because the wretched thing is to be carried in all weathers and into battle. Your pretty silks and satins would not last five minutes.'

Bess pulled a face and turned to look out of the window.

'They've been at it for hours,' she said. 'Do you suppose they're getting any better?'

Perdita threaded her needle into the fabric and laid it aside. She propped her elbow on the window ledge and leaned her chin on her hand.

On the forecourt, Adam Coulter stood with his hands on his hips, Simon beside him. Their backs were turned to the house, their sodden hats dripping water on to their buff leather coats.

Adam barked an order, and as one the little band of militia executed a left turn, pikes swaying and at least two of the farm hands half a beat behind the others.

'I suppose they are,' she said. 'Adam Coulter certainly seems to have more success with them than Simon did.'

'Well, he's a soldier. You'd expect him to know what he is doing,' Bess agreed. 'I must say, he's quite pleasing really. Not that I really like dark haired men.'

'Bess,' Joan chided.

Bess shot her stepmother a sulky sideways glance. 'It's not as if there is a parade of young men to our front door, is there, Joan? I'm twenty-one and I shall be an old maid soon. Tell me, how old is Adam Coulter?'

Joan thought for a moment. 'He would have been thirty-two on his last birthday,' she replied.

'There, perfect,' Bess declared. 'What do you think of him, Perdita?'

'Me?' Perdita turned to look at Bess. 'I've scarcely had a chance to form an opinion.'

Privately she thought Adam Coulter exceeded Bess's description of 'quite pleasing'. The years of soldiering had left their mark on his face. A silvered scar about two inches long skimmed his right eyebrow, giving him a rather dangerous demeanour, but it was not just the physical marks. The dark, intelligent face had a wary look to it, as if ready to spring into action at the rustle of a leaf, and those grey eyes missed nothing, no nuance of conversation or indiscriminate flutter of a hand.

Bess selected another needle and under the pretence of resuming her task, settled in for gossip. 'So why did he go off to the Continent, Joan?'

When Joan didn't answer, Bess looked up and cast a Perdita an uncertain glance.

'Joan?' Bess prodded.

'I can't tell you,' Joan said.

'But we're family. Surely we have a right to know,' Bess wheedled. 'Did he kill someone in a duel?'

Joan looked up, the surprise on her face giving both women the answer before she spoke. Joan recovered her demeanour. 'Someone died,' she said. 'That's as much as I can tell you.'

Bess huffed out a sigh. 'Very well, then tell us why is his name Coulter when the rest of you are all Marchants?'

Joan cleared her throat. 'Adam is… ' She paused for a moment, her gaze drifting to a corner of the parlour. 'Adam is the baseborn son of my brother, the late Lord Marchant. When Denzil was about three or four, my brother came home with a boy of a similar age and told us that he was the son of a woman called Ann Coulter who had died. As the child's father, he felt incumbent to take him and treat him as one of his own children.'

Bess set down her needle and put a hand to her mouth. 'How did his wife take it?'

A humourless smile lifted the corner of Joan's mouth. 'She was not amused and indeed when my brother was from home she spared nothing for the boy. Adam had a poor time of it. As Lady Marchant despised me equally, Adam and I became quite close. I couldn't protect him from her but I could provide something of a haven. We were both outcasts in my brother's home.'

Perdita glanced through the window at the man and wondered about the lonely child. Even from this distance the difference

17

between Simon and Adam couldn't have been more marked. Adam stood nearly a head taller than Simon and as lean as Simon was of middling height and stocky build. He held himself straight and still while Simon fidgeted.

'Small wonder you have no wish to return to Marchants,' Bess said. 'Does Lady Marchant still hold court there?'

Joan shook her head. 'No, she is dead these eight years past. Denzil's wife, Louise, is now Lady Marchant in her place.' Joan's mouth tightened. 'Louise is no better. My brother secured places at court for both boys. Denzil as a page and later a member of the royal household. He sent Adam to be a soldier in the King's life-guard.' Joan smiled. 'You wouldn't have recognised him then, quite the darling of the fine court ladies, but it all ended badly. Denzil and Adam fell out and Adam left court to avoid a scandal. Last I had heard he took up arms in the Continental wars.' Joan glanced out of the window, her gaze falling on her nephew's straight shoulders. 'And now he has come home. Why do I feel trouble will follow him?'

'But it sounds like he and his brother are reconciled,' Bess observed.

Joan scoffed. 'Denzil would only have attempted a reconciliation if he thought he could get something useful from Adam. Now Adam has turned him down, I don't expect any love to be lost between them in the months to come.' She clapped her hands. 'Now we really must get this banner finished in time for the muster.'

'They're definitely improving.' Simon sounded more hopeful than realistic.

Adam crossed his arms and thought for a long moment before

he replied. 'There is some improvement,' he conceded without much enthusiasm. 'You there...'

He abandoned Simon and strode over to a young lad of about nineteen whose pike waved about in an uncontrolled fashion, causing his fellow pikemen to jump away from him as it threatened to skewer them.

'Lad, you've a troop of enemy horse bearing down on you at the gallop, you have to stand firm. Wedge the end into the ground like so.' Adam demonstrated, whacking the end of the pike into the ground so firmly that a shudder ran up the stave of the ancient weapon and it cracked and splintered in his hand. He swore volubly and dropped the broken weapon as the blood welled from a cut on his hand.

Simon ran over to him, blanching at the sight of welling blood. 'You need to see Perdita,' he said. 'She's very good with this sort of thing.'

Adam wrapped a none-too-clean cloth, proffered by the boy whose pike had splintered, around the gashed hand and stomped back to the house, a wave of depression washing over him. If Simon Clifford paled at the sight of blood, God help him in the heat of battle.

He found Perdita Gray standing in the doorway waiting for him.

'I saw what happened,' she said. 'Come to my stillroom and I'll dress it for you.'

The door to the stillroom stood open and he paused in the doorway as she gestured for him to enter, saying she would return shortly with water and cloths.

The little room had once, in times long past he supposed, probably served the household as a chapel. Still visible behind the shelves and the neatly packed jars and pots, faded, peeling murals of biblical scenes could still be discerned. Sunlight, breaking through the grey clouds, streamed brokenly through the mullioned glass of the high window and fell on the bench, illuminating briefly the figure of Lazarus rising from the dead on the wall above her.

'Sit down and I will see to your hand.'

Adam started and turned to see Perdita in the doorway. He'd not heard her return.

He pulled a rueful face as he perched on one of the tall stools she used at her bench. 'I swear those pikes must have last seen service in the days of King Richard.'

She set the pitcher and cloths down on the table and busied herself selecting a pot from the row on the shelf above the bench.

'Quite likely.' She found the pot she sought and turned to look at him. 'Simon pulled them off the wall of the great hall. Now let's see to that hand.'

In the few days he'd been at Preswood, he'd had little opportunity to speak with Perdita. In the company of her kin, she kept herself apart, a silent, watchful presence as Simon and Bess chattered. He caught Joan glancing at her every now and then and wondered what it was about Perdita Gray that prompted the frown that creased his aunt's brow.

She pulled the matronly and unbecoming cap from her head and threw it on the bench in a crumpled heap as she unbuttoned her cuffs and rolled up her sleeves. She had tied her hair roughly back from her face in a loose knot and strands of nut-brown hair fell around her oval face.

Obediently he held out his hand, wincing at her gentle but sure touch. She glanced up anxiously and he smiled.

'It's fine,' he said, earning a small, quick smile from this strangely silent woman.

Perdita cleaned the cut across his palm, extricating several splinters of wood. He looked down at the glossy brown head, bent over in concentration.

'Ouch,' he said as her probing touched a nerve.

She looked up and shook her head. She had a perfect oval face, high cheekbones and large brown eyes, but her eyes had a wariness to them. Perdita Gray did not trust people easily and he had yet to win that trust.

'For a man who professes to be a soldier, you're not very brave,' she said.

'You have a deft touch, Mistress Gray,' Adam replied.

'My father was an apothecary,' she said. 'He let me help him. Had I been born a boy, I would have liked to follow his profession. It was my misfortune to be a girl. There, you'll live,' she announced. 'Now I'll just dress that cut.'

She unstoppered the jar she had chosen and sniffed the contents. 'This may sting a little,' she said, 'but it is most efficacious in healing wounds.'

'You're a Londoner from your voice,' Adam observed.

She looked up at him with surprise in her eyes. 'I am, although there is not enough gold in this country to ever induce me back into that accursed city.'

'Why is that?'

'I left my past behind me when I came to Preswood two years ago, Master Coulter.' She wrenched a clean cloth into strips of bandage and bound his hand. 'I thought I would be safe here but now there is all this talk...tell me, will this war reach us here?'

'No one is untouched by a civil war, Mistress Gray.'

She sat facing him, her hands folded in her lap. 'And you, Adam Coulter? What side will you take, or are you a mercenary who would sell his sword to the highest bidder?'

Adam felt an unexpected heat rise to his face. 'I can't deny that I fought in the German wars because it was employment, but if I choose to take up my sword in my own land, it will not be for that reason.'

'And what is your inclination?'

'I don't know.' He glanced up at Lazarus. 'I only know that the German wars taught me that in a civil war you can't stay neutral.

No matter how much it appals me, a choice will have to be made.' He brought his gaze back to meet her eyes again, wishing he could read the thoughts behind them, but no doubt years of long practice had given Perdita Gray a carefully controlled mask. He wondered what had happened to her in London that she had sought sanctuary in Preswood.

He continued, almost despite himself, voicing the thoughts that had been clashing in his head since he arrived back in England. 'God alone knows I didn't come home to take up arms in my own country against my own countrymen. I want no part of it.' His tone sounded harsh with emotion, even to his own ears.

'You're training Simon's militia precisely for that reason,' Perdita pointed out.

Adam shrugged. 'Unfortunately I am doing what I'm best at and that is a small thing I can do to repay his hospitality. It does not mean that I subscribe to your kinsman's politics.'

'Doesn't it?'

He rose to his feet and flexed the fingers of his damaged hand. 'We can pray that sense prevails and perhaps all this talk of war will be for nothing.'

'Perhaps,' she said, cocking her head to one side, her eyes searching his face 'But you don't believe that, do you? Now you must return to the pikes. Try not to get that bandage wet.'

'I will suggest Clifford has all the staves replaced.' At the door he stopped, turned and swept her a courtly bow. 'Thank you for your care, Mistress Gray.'

She responded with a curtsey and he thought he saw a glimmer of a smile twitch the corners of her mouth as she pulled up her stool to face the bench and opened a large leather-bound volume.

Adam hesitated at the door and looked back at her. She bent over the book, her slender fingers turning the pages as she unconsciously pushed her hair back, exposing the long, elegant line of her neck. Something jolted within him, something he had not felt in a very long time, an unfamiliar stirring of desire.

He wondered if Simon ever told her how beautiful she was.

He closed the door on the scene of domestic peace and strode back towards the Great Hall. A visitor had arrived and, engaged in the act of removing hat, gloves and cloak, he turned as Adam approached.

Robin's eyes widened in recognition. 'Adam? I would have thought you long gone from here.'

Adam took a breath to steady his nerves. 'What brings you to Preswood, Robin?'

'Denzil had received no reply from Joan so he sent me to ensure that the message had got to her.'

'Didn't Denzil trust me with his message?'

The colour rose to Robin's face. 'Yes, but—' He was saved from further explanation by Joan's appearance at the top of the stairs. 'Aunt Joan.' Robin took the stairs two at a time, bowing low and kissing his aunt's hand.

Joan looked up at her youngest nephew, holding him by the forearms as she studied him. 'Robin! It is you. My word you were but a lad when I last saw you. Now look at you. Whatever brings you to Preswood? Ludovic.' She addressed the steward who stood patiently holding Robin's outer garments. 'Some refreshment for our guest in the parlour, I think. Perdita, Adam, please join us.'

With her arm tucked into her nephew's she led her nephew away from the stairs towards the parlour.

Adam stood still watching as they rounded the corner away from his view. Joan saying, 'I do hope you can stay the night...'

'I heard voices.' Perdita's voice behind him roused Adam from his reverie.

He paused a moment before replying. 'My brother, Robin,' he said, attempting a lightness in his tone he didn't feel.

Perdita glanced up at him. 'Are you going to stand there all day? Or are you feared of facing your own brother?'

He straightened his shoulders. Perdita Gray seemed able to read his very thoughts. Yes, he admitted to himself, he was afraid of facing Robin. Denzil he could handle, but Robin had been only a boy when he had left England, a boy who had worshipped both his older brothers. Circumstances had now forced Robin to choose between them and, Adam admitted, the choice hurt.

'Perdita, please allow me to present my nephew, Robin Marchant. Robin, our kinswoman, Mistress Gray,' Joan said, the pleasure of the reunion written on her face. Perdita now wondered how the pain of the long estrangement from her family had affected Joan.

As they were introduced, Perdita scrutinised the young man's face searching for some likeness to Adam, but Robin Marchant bore no resemblance to his half-brother. He seemed impossibly young, not much older than Bess. His thick, auburn hair curled to his shoulder, his clothes were of good cloth, fashionably cut, and the lace on his collar looked expensive. He had an attractive, fine-boned face with lively, hazel eyes.

His mouth curled naturally into a smile at her entry; the smile of a man who liked women and knew that they liked him.

He bestowed the same winning smile on Bess who stood beside her stepmother, regarding the newcomer from beneath coy, fluttering eyelashes. Perdita was not fooled. As the first eligible young man to cross their doorstep for a long time—and a handsome one at that—Bess could be forgiven for a little harmless flirting.

'You are most welcome to Preswood.' Perdita dropped a dutiful curtsey. 'Forgive my curiosity but what brings you here?'

'Denzil didn't trust me to deliver his message,' Adam growled as he entered the room behind her. He strode over to the window and stood with his hands behind his back, looking out over the green where barely an hour previously he had been drilling Simon's militia.

Robin shot a quick glance at Adam's back before turning back to his aunt. 'Denzil wanted to be certain that you would be safe in the coming conflict, Aunt, and as he had not had a response from you he sent me to ensure that the message had been received.'

'I'm flattered that Denzil found it necessary to send two emissaries on that mission,' Joan said, 'particularly as no Marchant has shown the slightest interest in my welfare over the last ten years.'

Robin flushed. 'Father—'

'Yes, I'm quite aware of my brother's capacity for holding grudges, Robin,' Joan said. 'He's dead and now Denzil is trying to mend the bridges. How very commendable. Please thank your brother for his consideration, but Preswood is my home and I have no intention of leaving.' She paused, as if to compose herself. 'How is Denzil?'

'He is colonel in the King's horse,' Robin said.

'And you?'

'He made me a lieutenant,' Robin replied with the smile of a young man bestowed with great responsibility.

'And where is Louise in all of this?' Joan enquired.

It seemed to Perdita that the tension in the room heightened, crackling at the very mention of Lady Marchant's name.

Robin cleared his throat. 'Louise remains with the queen in France,' he replied. 'The queen is raising money for the King's cause, a cause we all hold dear.'

'Indeed we do,' Bess agreed.

Robin rose to his feet and faced his brother's stiff back. 'Well, Adam?' The challenge in his voice was unmistakable. 'Have you decided what side you take in the coming conflict?'

There was a brief, awful silence as Adam turned to face his brother, his shoulders rigid and his mouth a hard line. The contrast between this hardened soldier and the younger man could not have been more marked.

'Parliament has my sword, Robin.'

Robin gave a snort of anger, the fingers of his left hand resting on the hilt of his sword clenched and unclenched.

'I knew it. You have no loyalty, Adam. Not to yourself, your family or the king you have served. I should run you through now and save the king the trouble,' he blurted with the bravado of a school boy.

'I owe my family precious little loyalty, Robin.' Adam said sharply. 'Now, take your hand from your sword. It ill behoves your aunt's hearth.'

Robin flushed and dropped his hand to his side where his fingers twitched as if they longed to take to the sword again.

'Adam's right.' Joan's sharp voice interposed. 'I'll not have the first blood of this accursed war shed on my hearth. Keep your peace in this house, Robin.'

Robin looked down at her. 'For your sake, Aunt, but do not ask me to make peace with this man.'

'I don't,' Joan said quietly. 'I just ask you to mind your manners.'

'Robin.' Adam raised his hands in a conciliatory gesture. 'My past is tied with Denzil, not with you. Don't let us part this way.'

Robin's lips tightened. 'The king's enemies are my enemies,' he said and turned to his aunt. 'We believe the king will make his base in Oxford and I will make it my business to see you as often as I can, Aunt. For now I must leave you. While Adam remains here, I'll not stay.' He picked up her hand and kissed it. 'Until next time.'

Joan laid a hand, crooked with the arthritis that plagued her, on his head. 'God keep you safe, Robin. I am sorry you missed Simon. He had some business on one of the farms that called him away.'

Robin managed a faint smile and turned to Bess. 'Mistress Clifford, it has been a great pleasure to make your acquaintance, however brief.' His hand lingered on Bess's outstretched fingers slightly longer than propriety demanded as he added, casting a dark look at his brother, 'I apologise for the unseemly row.'

He briefly acknowledged Perdita's existence with a cursory bow and left.

Long after his footsteps had died away and the great door had shut, the silence in the parlour remained a palpable force.

'Is it true?' Joan spoke at last, her eyes fixed on Adam as they had been from the moment he had uttered the fateful words. 'Have you given your sword to Parliament?'

Adam returned her gaze without blinking. 'When I was in Stratford, Lord Brooke offered me a commission to join the garrison at Warwick Castle. I said I would think on it and I've made my decision.'

Joan lowered her head, the dark curls, liberally sprinkled with grey, hiding her face. 'Oh, Adam,' she said quietly. 'It shouldn't have come to this. To deliberately set yourself against your brothers...'

He crossed to her and hunkered down to her level, lifting her chin with his fingers so she looked into his eyes. 'I'm sorry, Joan, but I had to choose one side or another.'

Joan raised her head. 'I don't doubt your choice, Adam. It would not have been a decision made lightly.'

Adam laughed without humour. 'Like Robin, it will mean that I will be close by at Warwick, Joan.'

Joan shook her head. 'So with a nephew in both camps I should be kept quite safe.' Her voice dripped with irony. 'But it may have been better if you were as far away from here as possible. If the king is at Oxford, it will mean a dangerous proximity to Denzil.'

'I think Denzil is the least of my worries.' Adam sighed and rose to his feet. He looked around the pleasant room, his gaze resting momentarily on Perdita before turning back to his aunt.

'I will not abuse Simon's hospitality any longer. It is time for me to leave.'

'The war has not begun yet,' Joan said. 'You are welcome to stay as long as you wish.'

'No. I will seek out Simon on his return and tell him of my decision and then I'll be gone,' he said. 'I cannot in all good conscience remain here.'

As he passed her, Perdita caught at his sleeve. He looked down at her hand resting on his arm.

'Mistress Gray?'

She wanted to tell him that he was making a mistake and neutrality could be a possibility. What was there to prevent him continuing with his plans and taking up the property in Shropshire? If this conflict were to come to pass, it would happen with or without his involvement.

Their eyes met and she saw in the set of his jaw and the grey eyes that ran the colour of a stream in winter, that any form of remonstrance would be in vain.

'Nothing.' She released his arm and looked away as he strode out of the room.

Adam waited until Simon returned and went in search of his host. He found Simon standing at a table in the room Simon called the library, a sheaf of papers in his hand and a frown creasing his forehead.

'Am I interrupting?'

Simon looked up and laid the papers down. 'No. Not at all. Just looking at the cost of properly equipping my men.' He waved a hand at a tray with a flagon and glasses. 'Pour us both a glass of wine, Coulter. It's been a long day.'

Adam obliged, handing Simon a glass.

Simon sank down in his chair and raised his glass. 'Good news, I've had word from Northampton today. We ride to his muster in two days.'

'We?' Adam raised an eyebrow at the use of the plural.

'I'm being presumptuous, Coulter. I like you, my men like you, will you...will you join me?' Simon asked.

Adam swallowed. 'You've offered me friendship,' he paused, 'but my first loyalty must be to my conscience and I cannot support the King in this venture.'

Simon frowned. 'I don't understand.'

Adam took a deep breath. 'I've seen with my own eyes the evil the King has wrought on this land and I cannot share your faith in the rightness of his cause. I believe he alone has brought this country to the brink of war.'

Simon blinked. 'You're espousing Parliament?'

Adam inclined his head. 'Lord Brooke offered me a commission. I will leave tomorrow morning to accept it.'

Simon sat back in his chair. 'Oh,' he said. The confusion in his eyes made Adam realise that Simon had assumed that friendship would be enough. 'Is there nothing I can say that will dissuade you?'

Adam shook his head. 'No.'

'I cannot deny any man the right to his own conscience but I'm sorry that it has come to this.'

'So am I.'

Adam turned away, going to stand at the window looking out over the peaceful green fields and coppices that would soon be torn apart by strife. Simon stood up and came to stand beside him and the two men stood for a long moment in companionable silence.

'You've seen things that few men should ever be privy to,'

Simon said at last. 'I don't doubt the truth of what you say, but this thing is already too great to stop.'

'And it will carry this country with it.'

'Truth is, for all my fine words I've no great wish to leave my home and go and fight my fellow Englishmen.'

'Then don't.' Adam glanced at Simon, a man who he would have liked to call his friend. 'Stay and defend your home.'

Simon ran a hand through his sandy hair. 'It's not so simple. I swore an oath to Northampton and I'm honour-bound to keep it. I would not be called a coward.'

'Deciding not to fight is not a coward's choice, Clifford.'

'But breaking my word is a question of honour. I thought you might understand that.'

'Ah, honour,' Adam said. '"*Mine honour is my life; both grow in one. Take honour from me, and my life is done.*" Your own Shakespeare understood better than I.'

'I wonder what our Shakespeare would make of all of this?' Simon mused. He glanced at Adam. 'You'll be at Warwick with Brooke?'

'I believe so.'

'Then may I ask one boon of you?'

'Of course. Whatever is in my power.'

'If you have occasion to pass by Preswood can you ensure that all is well?'

'Of course,' Adam said. 'You have my word on that. It is the least I can do and my own kin is here. I could do nothing less.'

'Good,' Simon held out his hand. 'I'm sure, and I pray heartily, that this matter will be resolved by Christmas without recourse to bloodshed.' He hesitated. 'In the meantime, God keep you safe.'

Adam took the man's hand. 'And you.'

'You're leaving now? I thought you would wait 'til morning.'

Adam looked up from saddling Florizel, a handsome bay gelding he had bought in London. Perdita Gray stood at the entrance to the horse stall, one slender hand resting on the gnarled wood of the column.

'There is still sufficient daylight and I decided there was nothing to be gained from waiting until the morning, Mistress Gray. Everything has been said that needs to be said.'

'I wish you could have persuaded Simon from this course.'

Adam shook his head. 'Simon must deal with his own conscience as I must deal with mine.'

'I think he sees only glory and honour,' Perdita said.

'He will find the reality rather less to his taste,' Adam spoke without thinking and instantly regretted his words.

'What do you mean?' Perdita asked.

Adam leaned his head against the warm neck of his horse, breathing in the reassuring, familiar smell of horse and leather. Sense told him to hold his tongue but he found the words already forming as the scenes of those battles he had fought came flooding back.

'To ride into battle is to know real fear,' he said. 'Your bowels churn and your stomach is knotted hard. Your mouth is like dust. As the order comes to charge, you forget what cause it is you are fighting for because now the fight becomes your cause. Your fight is for survival. Around you men are dying in ways even your most harrowing nightmares could not have envisioned. There is smoke, confusion, and the smell of powder and of fear and blood and all around the screams of the dying. And when it is done, when you have survived and you are so tired you cannot even lift your head, then you want to weep. There is no honour in battle, no glory.'

'And when the enemy may be the man with whom you supped only the week before?' Perdita said.

Adam closed his eyes. 'That is the tragedy of civil war.'

He pushed himself away from his horse, making a show of buckling his bag to the saddle. When he found the courage to look up, he found Perdita's unblinking gaze fixed on his face, an unspoken grief written in her brimming eyes and tightly -held mouth. Shame at having been the cause of her distress washed over him. He wanted to take her in his arms and kiss away the tears.

'I'm sorry. I spoke without thought.'

'No.' Perdita straightened and looked away with an audible sniff. 'You spoke the truth and I'm glad for it.' She looked back at him and her brown eyes, fierce with understanding, held his for a moment. 'God speed you, Adam Coulter.'

He led the horse out into the courtyard and swung into the saddle. He looked down into the face of Perdita Gray and smiled. 'And God keep you safe, Mistress Gray.'

As he rode away from Preswood, the sun dipped below the horizon, casting long shadows over the immaculate lawns. He felt the cold shadow of premonition and shivered.

Chapter Four

'So when is this war going to start?' Bess asked blithely.

Simon, riding beside his sister, glanced at her. 'My dear sister, it already has.'

'Has it? How exciting.' Bess looked around at the peaceful fields slumbering in the summer sunshine as if she expected a troop of enemy horse to descend on them at any moment.

Perdita kept her attention on the road ahead. She took no joy in this excursion to Stratford where the Earl of Northampton had ordered a muster of the local militias, and she cast Simon a quick, affectionate glance. He rode at the head of his raggle-taggle tenants-turned-soldiers, one hand on his hip, resplendent in a new, stiff buff leather coat, his sword hanging from a handsome baldric, embroidered by his sister and stepmother, his hat sporting a jaunty red feather. Far from looking military and imposing, he looked like a small boy playing at being a soldier.

Simon's men plodded along in their wake, their voices lifted in the old soldiers' marching song. The banner she and Bess had stitched fluttered above them while they sang.

'Brave men in the field,
Their stout weapons wield,
With shining bright shields...'

In the same fields below Stratford where Lord Brooke had called a muster only a few weeks previously, Lord Northampton waited in a handsome marquee. Flags flew from the poles and a band played. Long trestle tables had been set up in the fields with abundant food for the men, and a sumptuous lunch had been promised for the officers and their ladies.

'Clifford, dear boy. You've done well.' The earl clapped Simon on the shoulder. 'Your men look splendid.'

Even Perdita had to concede that Simon's men looked the part in their uniform jackets of blue worsted, with the young black-smith's son recently promoted ensign carrying the banner at their head. The boy proudly placed the colours with an array of others and the men dispersed for their lunch and to partake of the free ale on offer.

Heads turned as Bess swept into the main tent. She had announced to Perdita that she had dressed with the intention of turning every male head in Stratford and it would seem she had succeeded. In deference to Simon's colours Bess wore a gown of peacock blue satin with a fine lace collar that barely disguised the low décolletage. Perdita's best gown of amber taffeta looked dowdy and puritanical in comparison.

'That dress is immodest,' Simon muttered as he took his sister's arm.

Bess turned innocent blue eyes on him. 'It's the latest fashion.'

'Well I don't approve and don't flirt like that.'

But Simon may as well have tried reproving the trees for all the notice Bess took of him. She intended to be the centre of attention and Simon had little choice but to abandon her to the droves of interested young men who circled her. Perdita sought refuge in a quiet corner and Simon went to fetch her a glass of wine.

'Stop smiling, Perdita. My sister is a disgrace,' he said, handing her the glass.

'Your sister is a lovely young woman who should be allowed a rare opportunity to enjoy herself,' Perdita replied. She took a sip of the wine and glanced down at the ruby liquid. Lord Northampton was clearly intent on impressing.

'Shall we circulate?' Simon suggested.

Privately Perdita just wanted to mount her horse and return home. The thought of having to make polite conversation with so many strangers filled her with dread, but she dutifully tucked her hand into the crook of Simon's arm and smiled and muttered polite inconsequential conversation with the other newly commissioned commanders and their ladies.

When Simon's turn came to speak with the earl, he left her with a final remonstrance to act as his sister's chaperone. She caught Bess's eye and gestured for her to rejoin her. With smiles and pretty waves, Bess shook off her admirers.

Bess scanned the room with a bright, excited gaze. 'Don't the men look fine?'

'They do,' Perdita conceded looking around the gathering of bright plumes and gold braid.

'What is it about men about to do battle that makes them seem so heroic?' Bess wondered aloud.

Before Perdita could reply she heard her name called and turned to see an unmistakable figure dressed in chartreuse satin, his hair curling past his shoulders and the beginning of a moustache on his upper lip, pushing his way through the throng. The other young men paled in comparison to Robin Marchant's good looks and Bess let out an audible sigh.

'Close your mouth. You look like a fish,' Perdita murmured.

'Do I look all right?' Bess fussed with her collar.

'You're perfect,' Perdita assured her.

Robin swept the ladies a deep bow and they both responded

with a polite curtsey. As he straightened, Perdita realised how tall
he was. Although she would have described Adam Coulter as well
above middle height, she recalled now that when she had seen
them together, Robin had topped his older brother by several
fingers.

'Mistress Clifford, Mistress Gray, what a pleasure to see you
both here,' he said with a smile, his gaze only for Bess.

'What brings you here?' Perdita enquired. 'I didn't think you
were with Northampton?'

Robin tore his gaze away from Bess and glanced around the
gathering.

'Denzil is here to talk with Northampton. I can't see him for
the moment.'

'You must introduce us,' Bess said. 'We would dearly love to
meet your brother.' She glanced at Perdita with a sweet smile.
'We've heard so much about him.'

Robin turned to peruse the crowd. 'Ah, there he is.'

As Robin gestured, a man pushed through the crowd towards
them. Perdita saw at once where Robin got his height. Denzil
Marchant was a big man both in height and breadth. His long,
strawberry-fair hair bristled around his face like a mane and he
affected a fashionable beard and moustache in emulation of his
royal master.

Adam Coulter bore little or no resemblance to either of his
brothers. Joan had described him as the cuckoo in the nest with
some justification.

'Rob. I've been looking for you,' Denzil boomed at his brother.
'My apologies, ladies. I didn't see you there.'

Robin turned to the women. 'My brother, Lord Marchant, may
I introduce Aunt Joan's stepdaughter, Mistress Clifford, and
kinswoman, Mistress Gray.'

'How does my aunt?' Denzil asked after the courtesies had been
exchanged.

'She's very well at the present,' Perdita replied. 'Although, as you probably recall, her health can be uncertain.'

Denzil frowned. 'She still suffers from that rheumatic fever?' When Perdita nodded, he said, 'I must pay a visit to her.' He looked around the company. 'Is your brother here, Mistress Clifford?'

'He is. He has raised a company of men for Lord Northampton,' Bess replied.

'Good to hear.' Denzil's face darkened. 'Now what's this Robin tells me about my scapegrace brother taking Parliament's shilling?'

'We believe he's with Lord Brooke at Warwick,' Bess said.

Denzil's moustache twitched, a crease deepening between his shaggy eyebrows. He shook his head. 'Brooke? So, it's true.'

Robin shrugged. 'I told you I had it from his own mouth, Denzil. Both these ladies were present.'

Denzil snorted. 'He's no blood of mine. I'll shed no tear when he's hanged as a traitor. Well, if you'll excuse me ladies, I have work to do. Robin, to me if you will.' He swept a bow and was gone, pushing his way through the crowd like a ship broaching the waves.

Robin glanced after his brother. 'My apologies, ladies. I am afraid that I too must abandon you.'

'So soon?' Bess could not hide her disappointment.

A smile lit Robin's face. 'I promise we will meet again soon, Mistress Clifford.'

He bowed low over Bess's hand, turned on his heel and disappeared into the press of people.

Bess sighed. 'Do you think he likes me, Perdita?'

Perdita laughed. 'I'm no judge of these matters, Bess.' She looked at her cousin's anxious eyes and smiled. 'But since you ask, yes, I do think he likes you.'

And why should he not? Perdita asked herself as a faint flush of pleasure rose in her cousin's face. Bess and Robin were both attractive people of the same age and station in life.

'There you are.' Simon, his face flushed and his collar askew, joined them. He fanned himself and huffed out a sigh. 'Warm in here. It's getting late and I must see you two safely home before dark.' As they walked back to the place they had left the horses, he asked, 'Have you had a pleasant afternoon?'

'Wonderful,' Bess said with feeling.

'What about you, Simon?' Perdita tucked her arm into his.

Simon turned a grave face to her. 'I will be marching with Lord Northampton in the morning.'

'So it begins?' Perdita said quietly.

He looked down at her. 'I fear so.'

Chapter Five

EDGEHILL. 23 OCTOBER 1642

B ess leaned her elbows on the bench of the stillroom, half-heartedly plucking the leaves off a stem of rosemary as she gazed up at the faded murals on the wall.

'Bess.' Perdita chided. 'Hurry up. I need those leaves.'

'Can you make love potions, Perdita?'

'Love potions? What nonsense are you talking? Would you have me burned as a witch?'

Bess sighed.

Perdita set down her pestle and regarded her friend. 'If you're thinking of Robin Marchant, I don't see any need of love potions there.'

Bess turned to look at her and Perdita had to smile at the bright, lovelorn eyes.

'Do you really think he likes me?' Bess asked, yearning in the droop of her mouth and anxious blue eyes.

Perdita laughed and shook her head.

Robin had ridden by two days previously with talk of battle and a wild look in his eye. Bess had given him a ribbon to wear as a favour. A blind woman could have seen that love potions were quite unwarranted.

The news he had brought was not quite so welcome. After raising his standard at Nottingham in August and an unsuccessful attempt to garner support in the north, the king had made his base in Oxford. That much Perdita had gleaned from Simon's regular, but brief missives.

'With the king based at Oxford, surely that brings this part of the country into great danger?' Perdita had asked Robin.

Robin shrugged. 'It won't be for long. The king intends to push through to London as soon as he can. Rest assured once he takes London that will be the end of it.'

'And what is there to stop him?' Bess had asked.

Robin shrugged, his eyes shining. 'The only thing between the king and London are the rebels at Banbury, but the Earl of Essex is marching as fast as he can to stop him. We expect fighting any day now.'

With that he had gone.

That night Perdita had studied a map in Simon's library. As her fingers traced the road to London and stopped on Banbury, she realised that their quiet corner of Warwickshire stood in the way. The fighting when it came would be on their doorstep.

Bess straightened, the rosemary falling to the table as she turned her attention to the open window. 'What's that noise? Can you hear it, Perdita?'

Perdita stopped and listened. Through the open window, above the sounds of the birds in the trees, came a faint, distant boom, like thunder in the clear sky.

'Cannon,' she said quietly. 'It must be cannon.'

Bess clutched at Perdita's hand. 'So close. I'm scared, Perdita.'

They listened and the sound came again. The ominous boom sounding like a knell on the peaceful life they had known.

Perdita thought of Simon, of Robin and, her breath stilled for a moment, Adam Coulter. Were they there on that field? Why would they not be?

She took a breath. 'We will need bandages, Bess. Lots of bandages.'

'What for?' Bess asked.

'Where there is fighting there will be wounded and with fighting so close I think we must be prepared.'

Bess stared at her as the reality of what the war could mean to them finally dawned on her.

'Wounded? Here?'

'Very likely. Don't just stand there, Bess, go and find those old sheets we set aside and join me in the parlour.'

Bess swallowed and did not move. 'Simon? Robin?' Her blue eyes brimmed with tears.

Perdita put her arms around the girl and held her. 'God will hold them safe,' she said. Poor comfort but all she had.

Adam shifted in his saddle and cast a sideways glance at the boy beside him. The young man was sweating profusely, probably a combination of nerves and the weight of the unaccustomed armour.

As the lad reached for his water flask and put it to his lips, Adam laid a restraining hand on his arm.

'Nay, lad. If you are thirsty, hold the water in your mouth and then spit it out. 'Tis not wise to go into battle with a full bladder.'

The boy looked at him with large, bright eyes and obediently took a swallow of water which he expelled on to the ground. He wiped his mouth and tightened his grip on the standard.

'Is it normal to feel sick, sir?' he asked at last.

Adam mustered what he hoped was a reassuring smile. 'Every man on this field would feel as you do.'

It had gone past noon and the whole morning had passed with both sides engaged in drawing up their forces on the slopes of Edgehill, near the village of Kineton. The king's forces had the advantage of the high ground, while parliament, under the Earl of Essex, stood with their backs to the village of Kineton. Adam with the cavalry was on the right flank of parliament's forces.

Florizel tossed his head and pawed the ground as if he were impatient to be getting on with business.

'Bloody amateurs.' This gruff comment followed by a voluble spitting sound made Adam turn in his saddle to exchange a glance with his sergeant, like himself a veteran of the continental wars.

'When did you last see action like this, sir?' the sergeant asked.

'Vlotho.' Adam replied.

Vlotho had been four long—very long—years ago. On that day he had charged behind Prince Rupert, son of the Elector of Palatine, a brilliant and volatile boy of eighteen. Now the same Rupert, nephew of the king, faced him on the slopes of Edgehill. Enemies where they had once been friends.

'I just wish something would happen.'

The boy beside him shifted awkwardly in his saddle. The sleeve of the arm holding the standard slipped back revealing a slender bracelet of plaited human hair, fair in colour.

'You've a sweetheart?' Adam asked to take the boy's mind off his increasing nerves.

The boy flushed. 'Aye, Jenny's her name. We were to be wed this autumn.'

Another wedding deferred by the war, Adam thought, thinking of Perdita Gray and Simon Clifford, whose betrothal he had walked in on. In the months since he had last seen Perdita he had willed himself not to think of her, but now the memory of the fall of her hair, the colour of age-darkened oak, set against the line of her long, pale neck as she bent over her book of receipts in her still-room, drifted into his mind.

'Sir?' The boy had asked him something and he had not heard.

'I'm sorry, lad. What did you say?'

'I asked if you had a wife, sir?'

Before Adam could answer, the ennui broke with the loud report of a cannon from the king's positions. An exchange from the parliament lines followed and the acrid smell of powder drifted across the field. The horses, unused to the noise, began to fidget, throwing their heads around and trying to back away.

Adam's horse laid back its ears, the whites of its eyes rolling as it tossed its head. He leaned forward and laid a hand on the high arched neck, whispering into its ear.

Beside him the young ensign, whose name he didn't even know, tightened his grip on the standard and took a great shuddering breath. From their left came a wild cry as the Royalist horse, led by Prince Rupert himself, leapt forward at the gallop. With whoops and shrieks they descended on the parliamentary cavalry with the impact of a blacksmith's hammer.

'Do 'ee see what I sees, sir?' The sergeant had come up beside him.

Adam nodded, his face grim. Part of the parliamentary line had turned on itself. There was betrayal in the ranks. The entire right flank of the line broke and fled, taking the closest infantry regiments with it.

'God 'ave mercy on us,' Adam heard the old veteran mutter as the royalist cavalry on the other flank careened down the slope of Edgehill in emulation of Rupert. Adam's troop of horse from the Warwick garrison had been placed under the command of Sir William Balfour, an experienced and wily old soldier. As Wilmot's charge began, Balfour gave the order to move his troops at a quick trot out of the range of the hallooing hordes.

Behind the cover of hedges, Balfour gave the order for his

troops to move up the hill toward the king's guns that belched fire and death on to the field below.

'What's happening, sir?' The ensign leaned forward, his face was now flushed with excitement.

'Balfour intends to silence the guns.' Adam replied, seeing the sense behind the old soldier's orders.

'Us? Take the guns?' Beneath the brim of his slightly too large helmet, the boy blanched and fell back from Adam to take his place in the line.

On the slope of the hill, still concealed by the hedges, Balfour drew his troops up to charge. At the point when the king's infantry had begun their advance under cover of the artillery, he gave the order to charge.

The bugles' blasts reverberated through the cold, clear air. Adam dug his heels into the sides of his horse, which responded by throwing back its back its head and leaping forward. The slender lines behind him responded and as a body they took the hedges and galloped toward the line of the king's guns and the centre of the king's infantry.

Rapidly discharging his pistols into a couple of unfortunate gunners, Adam drew his sword, his mind now totally centred on the task at hand. Overwhelmed by the unexpected press of man and horse, the king's guns fell silent and for the first time the parliamentary infantry moved forward to face a wavering, but stubborn, line of pikes and muskets.

It may have been four years since Adam had last seen battle, but the acrid smoke, the shrieks of the injured and dying, the rattle of muskets and the clash of steel on steel came back as if it were only yesterday. The politics that had brought these thousands of men to this quiet corner of Warwickshire ceased to matter. The struggle for mere survival overcame all normal senses.

'We've got the better of 'em,' the sergeant yelled above the noise. 'Hold yer ground, lads.'

'Wait,' someone cried. 'That's enemy horse heading our way.'

'Fall back.' The clarion call sounded across the field.

Adam lifted his head and cursed his commanders. They were so close to victory but the gloom of the autumn evening was drawing in and the royalist horse had begun to return to the field, blown and exhausted and hardly a threat.

There would be no victor, nor vanquished this day.

He looked around for the standard. The boy had fought well and maintained his grip on the rallying point. Now he saw him barely twenty yards away, engaged in a fierce dispute for possession of the colours. Adam turned his weary horse toward the boy's aid but it was too late. The sharp report from a pistol sent the young ensign jerking backward. He slid slowly from the saddle, the colours toppling sideways into the possession of a triumphant royalist.

The loss of the colours should have mattered but it didn't. Around Adam the fighting was ebbing as the soldiers of both sides fell back to their original positions. Adam slid from his saddle and knelt beside the boy, taking him in his arms.

Small bubbles of blood flecked the boy's lips. 'So cold, sir.'

Adam knew that the boy did not refer to the weather. 'It'll be a bitter night.'

'Did we win?'

'Yes.' Adam lied. 'You fought well.'

'Will you tell Jenny that?'

'Aye. I'll tell Jenny.'

The boy closed his eyes. 'So tired.'

'Sleep then.' Adam said softly and held the slight body until he sensed that life had fled. 'God forgive me, lad,' he whispered. 'I don't even know your name.'

With difficulty, he hitched the boy's body up over his saddle and leading both horses, made his way down the hill towards their original position to count the cost of the day and make plans for the following one.

As the first streaks of light illuminated the cold, grey, colourless morning, the wounded came. The echo of horses' hooves and the creak of wagon wheels sent Perdita hurrying downstairs. As she stepped outside, her breath frosted in the cold air and she shivered, thinking of the battle that had been fought the previous day and the wounded men who lay on the hard, frosted ground.

In the forecourt, a troop of horse, or what was left of a troop of horse, sat their weary mounts as their commander, a tall man on a bay horse, leaned down talking to Ludovic. Even in the grey light she could see from his build that it was not Simon and she slowed her steps.

As she approached him, the man raised his head, his fingers going to the brim of his heavy, iron helmet. She stopped, her breath catching. Adam Coulter.

She wanted to run to him, satisfy herself that he wasn't hurt, but even in the circumstances any undue haste could be construed as unseemly. Instead she raised her chin and walked purposefully across to him.

'Adam Coulter? What brings you here?

The answer was obvious and his red-rimmed eyes narrowed. 'I've wounded with me and I can take them no further.'

Perdita moved her gaze to the tired, dispirited faces behind him. Dreading what she might see, she turned to the wagons, recoiling momentarily from the stench of blood and worse and the piteous cries.

Adam swung himself down from his horse, wincing as he straightened his back.

Perdita caught the grimace of pain. 'Are you hurt?'

He shook his head. Beneath the shadow of the helm's brim, he looked exhausted, his face unshaven and grimy. 'Thank you for your concern, Mistress Gray, but no I'm not hurt. Just stiff. My men need rest and tending.'

'Take the wounded into the barn.' Perdita addressed an older man with a greying beard who seemed to carry some authority. She turned to Ludovic. 'See that there is food and drink for the men. I'll see to the wounded.'

She supervised the unloading of the wagons, hurrying ahead as the able-bodied men carried their injured companions into the grey stone solidity of the barn.

'We heard the sounds of the battle. Where was it?' Perdita threw the question to Adam as he helped one of the more lightly injured soldiers off his horse.

'Kineton village. A place they call Edgehill.'

Perdita drew in a quick, sharp breath. 'But that's barely ten miles from here. Who won?'

Adam shrugged. 'Both sides claim victory,' he said. 'The truth is neither.'

'How can that be?'

'When both sides lack the heart to finish what was begun, they can both claim victory, Mistress Gray.'

Bess emerged from the house carrying the basket of bandages and medical supplies they had assembled. She drew up short when she recognised Adam.

'Why did you have to bring them here? You're the enemy. You're not welcome at this house.'

Adam shot her a cold glance. 'This is war now, Mistress Clifford, and enemy or not, I have injured men. I knew Mistress Gray has some healing skills. Needs must.'

'Are you going to help, Bess?' Perdita asked.

Bess raised her chin. 'I'm a good Christian,' she said. 'Besides I ruined my hands preparing bandages yesterday so we may as well put them to use.'

'Then come with me.' Perdita laid an arm across the younger woman's shoulders guiding her toward the barn where upward of twenty men had been laid out on the hay. Some still groaned and cried out but most lay still and silent.

A man with a reeking stomach wound was carried past her. She took a step back her hand flying to her mouth.

'I can't,' she said. 'Perdita, I'm sorry but I can't help you. I think I'm going to be sick.'

Perdita retrieved the basket before Bess dropped it.

'You don't have to, Bess. Bring some food and drink, blankets and more bandages. Indeed, the contents of the stillroom.'

Bess turned and fled. Perdita walked the lines of injured making a rough assessment of who was in most urgent need of care. The injuries ranged from sword slashes to the horrific and there were some, such as the man with the stomach wound, for whom a speedy death was all that could be prayed for. It was indeed no sight for the fainthearted and her own stomach churned. Nothing in her experience had prepared her for this. The bloody, broken, stinking bodies were far removed from the day-to-day hurts of the farm workers or kitchen hands she was more used to tending.

She knelt beside a young man with a musket ball in his leg, helpless to know how to tackle such an injury.

'Let me, mistress.'

Ludovic appeared at her elbow. He laid a satchel down and took out a leather roll. He undid the lace and laid it out, revealing a set of bright, freshly honed knives and surgical instruments. Perdita picked up one of the knives, turning it over in her hand, and looked up at the man's broad impassive face.

'Ludovic these are surgeon's knives. How did you come by them?'

Ludovic shrugged. 'I was a surgeon's mate. The surgeon died of fever so I became the surgeon. The knives are mine. I feared this day would come so I have prepared.'

He set to work on the boy, with speed and appreciably more skill than any surgeon Perdita knew.

She passed him instruments as he asked for them with what seemed to Perdita no more than a flick of the wrist, he held up the musket ball. The patient gave a groan and fainted.

'Where are you from, Ludovic?' she asked as he stitched the wound

He did not look up from his work. 'My mother was Polish and my father Hungarian,' he said at last.

'You've not always been a servant, have you?'

'I've been a soldier and a sailor,' he answered. 'Your kinsman bought my freedom.'

Perdita knew that Geoffrey Clifford had travelled extensively in his youth and had returned to England with Ludovic as his manservant. There were stories that Clifford had purchased Ludovic in a slave market in Constantinople, but he had been part of the Clifford household for so long that no one thought to ask him about his origins.

'So, it was not just my uncle's story? You really were a slave?'

He paused and looked up at her, his expression bland. 'A galley slave, yes. The Turks took me in battle. I spent six years in the galleys until your uncle came across me in a slave market and gave me my freedom.'

'You were free and yet you chose to remain with him?'

His eyes never wavered but the hand holding the knife momentarily stilled.

'When you've been a slave, you know the value of choice.' He looked up at her. 'I think perhaps you of all people understand that, Mistress Gray.'

Perdita sat back on her heels.

When you've been a slave...

She'd never thought of it in those terms. Yet that is what she had been, bound to a man forty years her senior. When she had woken one morning and found him dead in the bed beside her, she had rejoiced.

As evening fell, Perdita sat with a dying man, his hand in hers. They had done what they could to repair the fatal slash to his belly, but he would be dead by midnight and his death would be a relief.

'Pray with me, mistress,' he whispered.

Perdita prayed and read to him from the Bible, straining her eyes in the poor light of the lantern.

'*You are my hope and my salvation...*' The familiar words mouthed by the dying man were surprisingly comforting.

She read until her voice cracked and the hand she held no longer sustained life. The man's eyes were wide open, staring with a look of peace as if he had indeed seen his hope and his salvation.

She closed his eyes and as she knelt over the dead man, tears spilling through her fingers, she felt a hand on her shoulder.

'You can't weep for them all, Perdita.'

She stood up, wiping her eyes on her grimy and blood-streaked cuff.

'How many, Adam?'

He shook his head. 'Probably thousands. Englishmen killing Englishmen.'

She looked into his tired, strained face. He hadn't left the barn once during the long day, choosing to stay with his men, keeping the dying company, talking with the lightly wounded. Now she could see he was at the end of his own resources.

He crouched down beside her and held out his hand. She took the slender love token of plaited hair curled in his fingers.

'He was only seventeen,' Adam answered her unspoken question. 'Tobias Clarke, son of the apothecary in Stratford they tell me. This was a parting gift from his sweetheart. I think he said her name was Jenny.'

Her fingers tightened on the circle of fair hair and she looked up at him, remembering the bright, cheerful lad who had served her in his father's shop. These were people she knew. It was one thing to mourn this man she had never known in life, but Toby She wondered if Jenny had been the pretty fair haired daughter of the innkeeper at the White Swan. She had seen the two of them, heads bent together in the intimacy of young love.

'Poor Jenny. Did she think it would make him immune from death?' she said, more to herself than the man beside her.

Adam raked his fingers through his hair. 'What do I say to his parents, Perdita? That he fought valiantly for the cause he so passionately believed in and he died defending his colours? That his death was swift and he felt no pain and that he is with God, rejoicing in the company of the saints?'

Perdita studied his face, the planes and shadows stark in the lantern light, hearing the bitterness in his tone.

'You don't believe in God, do you?'

His face stilled. 'I ...' He blew out a breath. 'I do not think God believes in me.'

She laid a hand on his arm. 'Come back to the house. You need food and rest.'

He nodded. 'I'm sorry to have troubled you here, Perdita. But I couldn't leave them to die like animals in ditches or on that field, and I knew that some would never make it back to Warwick.'

She shook her head. 'This is how it will be unless the differences between king and parliament are resolved, isn't it?'

He rose to his feet with a grunt. Holding out his hand, he

helped her stand. His strong fingers closed on hers, and lingered for a moment longer than propriety required. She shook her stiff limbs and together they walked back to the house.

At the foot of the stairs, Adam inclined his head. 'Goodnight, Mistress Gray. We will be gone in the morning. Thank you for the care of my men.'

'I did my Christian duty. Goodnight,'

She watched him as he followed Ludovic up the stairs as if it required every nerve of his body to stay upright. He did not look back, and in the morning he had gone.

Simon, his arm in a neat blue sling, came a few days later. There were shadows in his eyes that had not been there only weeks previously when he had taken his men to join Lord Northampton. Now he had seen battle and viewed the darkness of men's souls. Simon would never be quite the same man again.

Joan and Bess tactfully withdrew and left them in the gathering gloom before the fire in the great parlour. Perdita drew up a stool and leant her head against Simon's knee, thinking that this was how it should always have been, had it not been for a stubborn King or a man called Adam Coulter. She wondered where he had gone after he had left Preswood. Back to Warwick, she supposed.

Simon rested his hand lightly on her head, drawing her thoughts back to the present.

'You've not told me, how did you hurt your arm?' She asked the question Bess had posed on seeing her brother.

Simon had skilfully evaded an answer and now he gave a self-deprecating laugh. 'For you, sweetest, only the truth. My cursed horse caught a hoof in a rabbit hole and I went down in the first charge. My noble wound is, I fear, no more than a badly sprained wrist.'

'Thank God it was not your neck.'

'Indeed,' he agreed. The silence that followed, broken only by the crackling logs, seemed to stretch for an eternity until the intimacy of the fire and the good Rhennish that Ludovic had produced loosened Simon's tongue and he leaned back in his chair.

'I had no thought that men could die so many dreadful deaths, Perdita.'

Oh, Simon, dear good man, Perdita thought. She could see him sitting in the grass on the slopes of Edgehill, nursing his wrist while before him men and horses died.

'But you saw it too,' he continued. 'I hear Coulter came here after the battle with his wounded.'

'He did. I think it might in some ways be more merciful to die swiftly on the field than to die the lingering and horrible deaths I saw.'

'What became of the dead and wounded?'

'The three soldiers who died in the night were buried in the churchyard, their deaths recorded simply in the church records as *Killed in the Kineton fight*. Some were local men so they were returned to their families, the others still too sick to move we distributed among the village for care,' Perdita said.

Simon nodded. 'We must see that our people are compensated for their board and lodging,' he said.

'But they are parliament men.'

'They are men. It doesn't matter what colours they fight under.'

Perdita's heart swelled and she remembered why she had agreed to marry this good, decent man. She knelt up and laying her hands on his knees, she kissed him on the forehead. Simon groaned and, with his good hand, pulled her on to his lap, wrapping his arms around her, his breath coming in shuddering gulps as if emotion had completely overwrought him.

'They have stopped saying the thing will be done by Christmas,' he said at last. 'It's no little rebellion and now the King has missed his chance to regain London. I doubt there will be such an opportunity again.'

'And you, Simon?'

'Well, sweetest, I am committed now to see this thing through.'

'And us? Our wedding date?'

She knew the answer even before he spoke. 'I won't risk leaving you a widow to mourn at my grave side. Let us wait and see this thing through a few more months.'

She cupped his face in her hands and said fiercely, 'Simon, I would rather be a widow mourning at your graveside who has known some happy times with her husband than to mourn and wonder what might have been.'

He disengaged her, setting her back on her feet, taking her hands in his, he smiled.

'We'll see what the New Year brings, Perdita, but now is not the right time.'

Chapter Six

THE BATTLE OF STRATFORD, 25 FEBRUARY 1643

'I really don't think you should go to Stratford,' Joan protested from her bed. 'It isn't safe.'

'Nonsense,' Perdita said. 'Stratford is garrisoned for the king, and I encountered no difficulties last time I went there.' She laid a hand over Joan's crooked fingers, the joints swollen and hot from the rheumatic fever that had plagued the woman since her youth. 'We have no more laudanum and I am not going to let you suffer like this.'

Ignoring Joan's protests, Perdita, riding pillion behind Ludovic, set out on the five-mile ride to Stratford. They were less than a mile from the town when a crash like thunder caused the horse to shy, nearly dislodging Perdita. She twisted her hands into Ludovic's belt and righted herself.

'Is that guns?' she asked.

'Yes, mistress. We should turn back.'

'No. I must get the laudanum,' Perdita said. 'Ride on into town. The garrison's probably just practising with their artillery.'

The guns boomed again. Ludovic didn't move.

'Ludovic, go on, please.'

The manservant's shoulders rose and fell in a silent shrug of acquiescence and he urged the skittish horse forward.

As they approached Clopton bridge, another report of cannon fire sent the horse into a lather and it went down on its haunches, fighting the bit.

'Look, mistress,' Ludovic pointed at the town where smoke rose above the roofs. 'That's not target practice. There's fighting in the town. We need to find shelter before we become caught.'

Even as he spoke, yells and the report of musket fire came from the far side of the town. The melee grew louder, and as they crossed the bridge a tide of men appeared, running down Bridge Street towards them.

Ludovic dismounted and lifted Perdita down. Leading the horse, he pushed against the panicked soldiers. A couple of men, their eyes wide with fear, tried to grab the horse's bridle but Ludovic fought off their hands with his riding crop.

The doors of the townhouses were firmly bolted and the windows shuttered, and no one responded to Ludovic's knocking. They had no choice but to press on and find some sort of shelter. He led them into a narrow laneway between two houses near the Market Hall. He pulled a pistol from a holster on the saddle and holding the terrified horse, he placed himself between Perdita and the street.

Perdita flattened herself against the wall. Around his arm she could see the fleeing men, pursued by horsemen wearing orange sashes, and the source of the conflict became clear. The king's men were being routed from the town.

The fighting around the Market Hall grew fierce as the royalists within the buildings made one last stand. The horse broke free of Ludovic and took off into the street. Ludovic cursed and pushed Perdita down to the ground as musket balls whizzed over their heads, striking chips from the stone work above them.

Perdita crouched against the wall, trying to make herself as small as possible, her elbows pressed to her sides to stop the uncontrollable shaking. Part of her wanted to jump to her feet and run as far as she could reach, but she knew if she even tried to stand, her legs would fail her.

A massive explosion came from within the Market Hall, raining Cotswold stone, tiles and dust down on the two huddled figures. Perdita raised her head, her ears ringing, her lungs filling with dust. Great holes had been blown in the walls and fire blazed through the old hall. She could hear screams and through the smoke she could see men running from the building.

The explosion seemed to shatter the last of the resistance and the street began to clear, the orange-sashed horsemen slowing to a walk as they rounded up the surrendering royalists. Ludovic helped Perdita to her feet and she shook out her cloak and skirts, bits of stone and plaster falling to the cobbles.

A shadow darkened the entrance to their hiding place.

'You down there, come out at once.' A parliamentary officer on a bay horse sat looking down at them, his hand on his sword hilt, his face shadowed by the iron grille of his heavy pot helmet.

'We're not soldiers,' Perdita coughed. Her mouth had dried with fear and the clogging dust around them.

The soldier raised his hand from the sword and pushed the grille of his helmet back.

'Mistress Gray. Ludovic. What in God's name are you doing here, this day of all days?' Adam Coulter demanded. Perdita shook her head, trying to dispel the ringing in her ears. Adam's voice sounded as if it came from a long way away.

'Captain Coulter, thank the Lord.' Her knees buckled with the relief of seeing a familiar face and she had to steady herself against the wall as the world around her began to sway. 'I had to get laudanum for Joan. She's not well.'

He swung down from his horse and looping the reins around

his arm, put out his gauntleted hand to draw Perdita into the light. 'Your timing could have been better. Lord Brooke has just driven the royalists from the town.' His brows furrowed and he peered at her. 'Mistress Gray, you're hurt. You've blood on your face.'

Perdita put her hand to her face, the shaking fingers coming away sticky with blood, mingled with dust. 'Oh, you're right.'

The world began to roar and spin around her. She dimly heard Adam's voice calling for Ludovic before Stratford disappeared into a roaring abyss.

It had been a lovely dream of her first Christmas with the Clifford family at Preswood before the war. Geoffrey had still been alive and there had been singing and a yule log blazing in the hearth. Now the bright, cheerful fire faded and Perdita became aware of low voices around her.

'There now, she's coming around. I said it wasn't bad.'

She recognised the voice of the apothecary and opened her eyes, grimacing at the bright light. Adam Coulter's face, tense with concern, peered down at her.

'What happened?' she asked.

'A piece of stone must have hit your head,' Adam said. 'It's only a glancing blow but head wounds bleed like the devil.'

Perdita put tentative fingers to her head to encounter a bandage over a thick wad of padding at her hairline over her forehead.

'Ow. It hurts now,' she said. 'It didn't before.'

'Of course it hurts,' said the apothecary. 'You'll have quite a headache for a couple of days.'

Perdita tried to sit up but Adam's hand on her shoulder restrained her. 'You lie still.'

'But I've got to get Joan's laudanum and get home before dark.'

'Ludovic's dealt with that. God's death, Mistress Gray, what were you thinking? You shouldn't be riding around the countryside.'

'I wasn't riding around the countryside. I was on my usual business,' Perdita protested. 'No one told me there was going to be a battle in Stratford today of all days.'

'Remind me to consult you next time.' Adam smiled and his fingers brushed the bandage above her ear.

She wished he smiled more often. In the curl of his lips and the sparkle in the light grey eyes, she could see a passing resemblance to his brother, Robin. But where Robin still had the prettiness of youth, the hard planes of Adam's high cheekbones and strong aquiline nose marked him as a man who carried authority, a man she would trust without question. She imagined that he must be a good officer. She'd seen it in his men's eyes the day after Edgehill.

'You must have things to do,' Perdita said. 'I'll be just fine in a couple of minutes.'

Adam shrugged. 'Things are taking care of themselves. That's what sergeants are for.'

Perdita glanced at the window where a lowering sky presaged snow.

'I've got to get back to Preswood.'

'You are going nowhere,' the apothecary said.

'Ludovic tells me you lost your horse, so he has set out for Preswood on foot with the laudanum, but you are spending the night in Stratford,' Adam said. 'I'll take you home in the morning if you are up to the ride.'

Perdita opened her mouth to protest but even as she tried to rise, the world tipped and swayed.

'My wife's made up a bed for you, Mistress Gray,' the apothecary said.

Before Perdita could protest, Adam had picked her up bodily.

'Not exactly a feather,' he grumbled, and laughed as the heat rose in Perdita's face. 'That's better.'

He carried her up the stairs and deposited her on the bed Mistress Clarke had made up.

'She'll be fine with me, Captain Coulter.' Mistress Clarke bobbed a curtsey.

Adam smiled down at Perdita. 'I'll see you in the morning.'

As the door shut behind him, Perdita struggled to sit up.

'Let me help you, Mistress Gray.' The goodwife's quick fingers tugged at the laces of Perdita's bodice. ''Twere madness to come to Stratford today of all days,' she said.

'I didn't know there would be a battle,' Perdita pointed out, 'and Joan Clifford is ailing and needed the laudanum.'

'Aye, well 'tis lucky Captain Coulter found you when he did.' She tutted as she held up Perdita's collar, liberally stained with blood. 'I'll put that on to soak, and your cuffs too.'

The woman paused in her ministrations and looked around the little room. 'This was Tobias' chamber,' she said. 'You know he died?'

'Yes,' Perdita replied, lying back on the bed. 'Captain Coulter told me. I'm sorry.'

'He's a good man, Captain Coulter,' Mistress Clarke said. Her mouth tightened but the betraying tears rose in her eyes and trickled down her plump cheeks. She sat down on the bed with a thump and Perdita laid her hand on the woman's arm.

'Foolish of me,' the woman said. 'Captain Coulter wrote such a lovely letter about how brave Toby had been and how he hadn't suffered ... at the end.'

Remembering Adam Coulter's bitterness at Tobias' senseless death, Perdita kept her peace and the woman drew a deep, shuddering breath and rose to her feet, wiping her eyes on her apron.

'Now you rest. My John has left a draught for you to help you sleep, should you need it.'

But Perdita's eyes were already closing.

When Adam returned to the apothecary's house in the morning, he found Perdita up and dressed and partaking of a breakfast of gruel. Beneath the white bandage that circled her head, her face seemed drained of colour and there were dark circles like smudged bruises around her eyes, but she greeted him with a smile that lit her face ... and his heart.

'Are you sure you can be spared? Perdita asked him.

'I'm sure. I've no pillion saddle but I've a sturdy horse.'

He lifted her on to the saddle and swung up behind her across the broad withers of Florizel. He looped the reins around her, drawing her in against him. Her slight figure fitted well into the circle of his arms as if she had been made to fit. Only she hadn't, he reminded himself, she belonged to another man.

As Florizel took his first loping steps, Perdita stiffened, her hand going to the bandage around her head.

'Are you up to this?' Adam enquired.

Her shoulders squared. 'I'll be fine. There is no need for you to be concerned.'

'There's every need. The countryside between here and Banbury is overrun with the rabble from Stratford and they will be undisciplined and lawless.' He huffed out a sigh. 'You were lucky, Perdita. Very lucky. When I think about what could have happened.'

She lowered her head, offering him a tantalising view of her elegant neck brushed with dark curls.

'I know that now, but Joan needed me.' She laid her head against the heavy leather of his buff coat and closed her eyes. 'Why did the Market Hall explode like that?'

'We think they were storing powder there and a spark caught. But enough talk of war, we have an hour in each other's company. Let's talk of other matters.'

She glanced up at him. 'What other matters?'

He mused for a long moment and asked the question he had longed to ask since he had first met her.

'Tell me how you came to Preswood?'

'I had nowhere to go.' He caught the strain in her voice as if it were almost too much to relate. 'My husband's debts had taken all my jointure. His family turned me out.'

'Your husband?'

'Samuel Gray. My father sold me to him when I was but sixteen and he a man near sixty.'

The enormity of what she was saying hit Adam like a jolt. A girl of sixteen forced into marriage with a man forty years her senior?

'Had you no say in the matter?'

She shook her head and flinched, her hand going to the bandage. 'My dear father beat me and starved me into submission,' she said. 'What choice did I have?'

None.

A growing well of anger rose in Adam's chest. If he were to meet Perdita's father...

'And your father could not help you when this husband died?'

'He had died two years earlier. His business had been sold. I had no other family to turn to except my mother's kinsman, Geoffrey Clifford. He and Joan offered me a home without condition. Whatever I lacked in love or family, they more than made up for.'

Adam said nothing for a long moment. Joan would always be the one who took in orphaned kittens, stray dogs or injured wildlife — or unhappy children. She would not have hesitated to take in this lost waif and given her the love she needed to heal. Was that why Perdita had agreed to marry Simon? Was it gratitude?

He changed the subject. 'How did you come to be called Perdita?'

She shrugged. 'I don't know. A fancy of my mother's. I looked for the name in the Bible but I couldn't find it there.'

He laughed. 'The Bible? You'll not find it there. Perdita is a character from a play by Shakespeare.' He glanced behind him at the receding church tower of Holy Trinity. Shakespeare's burial place, they said.

'Is it? A play? Truly?' She twisted to look at him. 'I've not read any of his plays. My father and my husband did not approve of such things. What play is it?'

'A Winter's Tale,' Adam said. 'Perdita was the daughter of the king and queen. It would mean 'lost', if my Latin serves me correctly.'

'Lost?' Perdita repeated vaguely. 'Is that me? Am I lost? It seems that we share something in common.'

His breath caught. 'What is that?'

'We have both been lost, have we not?'

He considered that question. 'But you at least have found where you belong,' he said. 'I am still looking.'

He remembered the property in Shropshire the London lawyer had sent him to look at. That had been an illusion, an impossible dream. There was nowhere in this benighted kingdom he would probably ever call his own.

She leaned her head back against his chest and closed her eyes. A twinge of panic caused him to put his heels to Florizel to spur the plodding gait of the horse. Surprised by this unwanted attention, Florizel jerked and Perdita's eyes opened.

'Something wrong?'

'Nothing. Florizel must have seen a hedgehog,' Adam said. 'Not far now.'

As she drifted off again, he tightened his arms around her, telling himself that he didn't want to risk her falling from the saddle, but knowing his motives to be something else entirely. She felt right in his arms and he wanted the moment never to end. But even as that traitorous thought crossed his mind, the gates of Preswood loomed ahead of them.

He shook her awake. 'Home,' he said.

'Already?' She almost sounded disappointed, and as if remembering her manners, asked, 'Will you stay for a little while?'

He shook his head. 'No, I have to be back at Warwick as soon as I can.'

'When will I see you again?'

Did he detect a soft note of longing in her voice or was he imagining it, imposing a wish on her that was not in her heart?

'I don't know, Perdita,' he said in a low, tight voice.

'Adam Coulter,' she whispered.

'Perdita Gray?'

'Nothing,' she said. 'It's a nice name.'

He pulled himself together. 'That bang on the head has addled your senses, Mistress Gray.'

'I haven't thanked you,' she said.

'No thanks are required.'

'Please stay.'

'I can't. God keep you safe.'

She closed her eyes and smiled. 'You don't believe in God.'

'I told you, he doesn't believe in me.'

Adam was spared from further conversation by the sight of Ludovic waiting at the front door.

'Ah, Ludovic. Here is your mistress safe and well.'

He lowered Perdita into Ludovic's waiting arms.

'Mistress Clifford would see you, sir.'

He nodded and swung off the horse.

Joan lay in a large bed, propped up by bolsters. A smile lit her thin face at the sight of him and she held out her hand to him. He

AND THEN MINE ENEMY

took it gently, mindful of the swollen and crooked joints that pained her.

'Adam, thank the Lord, you found Perdita and returned her to us safe and well.'

'She's had a bad knock to the head but nothing a few days rest won't put right.'

Joan nodded. 'Don't fret over Perdita,' she broke off, her eyes narrowing as she scanned his face. 'Adam, is there something you're not telling me?'

He shook his head. 'Nothing, Aunt. I am sorry I cannot stay longer. I am expected back at Warwick today.'

He bent his head and kissed her cheek, cool and dry beneath his lips. He breathed in the familiar scent of lavender that had been part of his earliest memories of this woman who had been his greatest friend and ally.

'Joan,' he whispered, leaning his forehead against hers. 'Don't leave me, not when I've only just found you again.'

'Silly boy,' she chided, resting her hand on his cheek. 'Go, now. Duty calls.'

Chapter Seven

The route between Gloucester and Warwick had become a vital supply route for the parliament forces in the Midlands and north, and of all the tedious jobs that fell to him, Adam most disliked convoy escort. Although it got him out of the stultifying tedium of garrison duty, the task could be at the same time both mind-numbingly boring and nerve- racking. Running so close to the king's headquarters at Oxford and the royalist garrison at Banbury, the convoys were under constant threat of attack, and in the shuffling campaigns of the early summer, the king's troops were particularly active.

Adam had collected a convoy carrying cloth for much needed uniforms at Gloucester. He took the precaution of splitting it into three separate parties, sending two by different routes. If one were to be attacked, then there was a smaller risk of losing the entire shipment. However, it meant spreading his men across the three shipments and risking the defence of the wagons.

The rain that had begun as he left Warwick had been unforgiving and the roads had worsened under the continual soaking.

Adam sat his horse, feeling rain drip from his helmet down the back of his neck as a wagon driver, mired up to his knees in mud, cursed and swore at the oxen who refused to move. They were still six miles from the relative safety of Stratford and he had no desire to be caught in the open by a superior force.

'This is taking too long,' he muttered to his sergeant.

The sergeant grunted in agreement. 'You lads,' he indicated three of the troopers. 'Get down there and help that fool.'

The troopers looked at him with distaste. 'In the mud, sergeant?' one ventured.

'Yes, in the mud, you pack of dozy milkmaids.'

Grumbling, the troopers dismounted and reluctantly went to the aid of the beleaguered wagoner.

'Cap'n!'

Adam looked up as one of his scouts careened down the road towards them.

'Soldiers, sir. King's men,' the scout announced, his breath coming in short gasps from his exertion. 'About forty horse.'

'Where, you fool?' Adam had no time for such vague information.

'There.' The boy pointed with a shaking finger at the rise of the hill before them.

Adam cursed.

Adam's troops were hopelessly outnumbered by at least two to one, and he cursed both his decision to split his force and his commander's miserliness at not providing him with the extra troops he had requested. Brooke would have seen them well provided for, but Brooke had died at Lichfield only a few weeks after the affair at Stratford and his successor, Purefoy, lacked his drive or brilliance.

Adam had no time to think further on the vagaries of his commander. His opponent had probably counted on catching them as they crossed the small, swollen river that stood between their current position and the line of horsemen now spread out across the hill. However, he had misjudged his timing and Adam's force was not in a bad position. The high hedges on either side of the road would hamper an attack by cavalry and the wagons provided an effective block. However, he barely had time to deploy his men into positions along the banks of the river before the King's men charged.

As the royalist troops approached, his heart sickened as he recognised the royalist commander. Denzil Marchant would have been unmistakable at any distance. He rode a tall, black horse and his scarlet and silver cloak, dark with the rain, flew out from his shoulders. Eschewing a helmet, he strongly resembled a Teutonic god bent on vengeance with his wild, red hair flying out behind him as he charged toward the waiting parliamentarians at a stiff canter. Fine sport for a summer's afternoon.

'Hold your ground,' Adam yelled and his men, whom he had spent the better part of the winter and spring training, obeyed, rattling off a volley of musket fire that brought down several of the enemy.

The impetus of the charge stalled and Denzil's men hesitated long enough for Adam's men to reload and get off a second volley.

Denzil, his teeth bared and his eyes wild, shouted something unintelligible and put his heels to his horse. The remaining men came after him and they hit the parliamentarians with the force of a hammer. Denzil at their forefront slashed down at the men on foot with his sword like a demon possessed. It was to Adam's credit that his men stood their ground before the force of numbers became too great and they fell back, despite Adam's attempts to rally them. He understood his men were not prepared to sacrifice themselves for wagons of cloth whatever its worth to their superiors and, recognising that a hasty retreat could also be in his own best interests, Adam turned to follow them.

As he wheeled, he heard the report of a pistol at close quarters.

Florizel screamed, rearing, his front legs paddling the air in agony as a second pistol discharged. Adam disengaged his feet from the stirrups and managed to throw himself clear as the horse fell to the ground. The fall knocked the wind from his lungs with the sickening crack of ribs.

Florizel continued to scream, with an almost human intensity and heedless of the figure on horseback looming over him, Adam's fingers scrabbled in the holster of his fallen mount. His second pistol, primed and unfired, was in his hand as Denzil shouted above the melee.

'Lay down your weapon.'

Adam forced air into his tortured lungs. 'My horse,' he said, and ignoring his brother, turned to his beloved bay gelding, which lay quivering in agony, his eyes rolling in terror and pain.

'Sorry, old boy,' he whispered in his ear as he put the pistol to Florizel's head, ending the animal's pain.

He stroked the animal's neck until the last of the life slipped away, and only then did he turn to face his brother, letting the pistol fall as he tried to stand.

To his surprise, his left leg refused to work. He fell back against the body of his horse and slid to the ground, his back against the dead animal. With curious detachment, he looked down at the blood welling darkly from a wound in his right thigh. He couldn't even recall being hit but now the pain flashed across his eyes in a red mist.

He looked up into Denzil's flushed and triumphant face.

'You always were a damned poor shot, Denzil,' he said as the world started to close in on him. Before he passed out, he thought he heard Denzil call his name.

When he came back to his senses, he lay flat on the ground. Someone had removed his helmet and rain spattered his face. He groaned as sensation in the form of a burning brand on his leg returned. He tried to sit up but a firm hand pushed him back down again.

'Lie still, damn it. You'll start bleeding again.' It was Robin's voice, annoyance masking a genuine concern.

Adam opened his eyes and swallowed back the bile that rose in his throat. 'Where's Denzil?'

'Counting his spoils,' Robin said. 'Our intelligence said twenty wagons and there are only six here. I take it you split the convoy?'

Adam managed a grim smile between gritted teeth. 'Now that would be telling.'

'Well, well. Adam Coulter.' Denzil's voice boomed from above him. 'A bloody rebel. Why am I not surprised.'

He squatted down and Adam saw no mercy or quarter in his brother's eyes. 'What am I going to do with you?'

'You're going to get him to a chirurgeon,' Robin interposed.

'Now, Rob, no need for haste. Adam is a damned sight tougher than he looks. He'll make it to Oxford before we need to bother with the surgeons. But before then he can tell us where the rest of the convoy is.'

Denzil rose to his feet and when Adam didn't respond, a well-aimed boot caught Adam's wounded leg. He rolled over, retching in pain.

Robin rose to his feet. 'Christ, Denzil. No prisoner should be treated that way.'

'He's the only one who can tell us where the rest of the convoy is.'

'Who cares? We have six wagons of stout cloth.'

'We wanted twenty.'

'Then send the men out to look for them. They can't be too far behind.'

'You are coming perilously close to insubordination, lieutenant.'

In the ensuing silence, Adam opened his eyes to see his brothers standing toe-to-toe over him. To his surprise, Denzil backed down first, turning on his heel and striding off, barking orders as he went. Robin squatted down beside him again.

'Damn it,' he muttered. 'The wound's bleeding again.'

'Is it bad?' Adam took a shuddering breath. It felt bad.

'The ball's lodged quite deep, I think. Heaven alone knows what it took with it. There's nothing more I can do. You really do need a surgeon.'

Adam grasped his brother's sleeve and hauled himself into a sitting position, wincing as he realised he had several cracked ribs to add to his misery. He leaned back against his dead horse.

'You've already done more then you needed. Denzil will do what he wants and neither you nor I can sway him. If he means to make me ride to Oxford, there is nothing I can do to persuade him otherwise. Except maybe die.'

Robin shrugged and sat down next to his brother with his arms across his knees. 'Damned weather,' he said. 'I thought the rain would let up by now, but I think it's just getting heavier.'

Denzil appeared again, rubbing his hands together in satisfaction. 'The king will be happy with this little lot,' he said. 'On your feet, Coulter.'

'I have a musket ball in my thigh, Denzil,' Adam pointed out.

'You're awake and talking so it can't be too bad,' Denzil said. 'Find him a horse, Rob. There are a couple of your men, Coulter, who won't be needing theirs anymore.'

'Denzil...' Robin protested.

'What are you waiting for, Rob? Go and find a horse.'

As Robin stomped away, Denzil crouched down beside his brother, studying Adam's face.

Adam sucked in his breath. His leg burned like the devil and he wondered how Denzil expected him to sit a horse.

'If I'd known it was you, I may have taken more trouble with my aim,' Denzil said. 'Louise will certainly not be pleased that I missed.'

'I don't doubt that. How is your wife, Denzil? Still generous with her favours?'

Denzil's eyes narrowed. 'Louise and I have an understanding.'

Adam was tempted to laugh but he knew that would hurt his injured ribs, and if he pushed his brother too far on the subject of his wife he risked another boot to his leg.

Further banter was spared by Robin, leading a dispirited nag that had no doubt belonged to one of Adam's troopers.

'All right, on your feet,' Denzil said.

Adam closed his eyes and willed himself to comply but his head spun at the thought of putting any weight on his injured leg, filling him with dread. He braced himself for another well- aimed boot from his brother, but it was Robin who bent down and, with his arm around Adam's shoulders, pulled him to his feet.

Upright, every nerve in Adam's body protested and the world began to lurch in an alarming fashion, but he forced himself straight despite the shafts of pain that suffused his body from his leg and the cracked ribs. He set his jaw. He would not give Denzil the satisfaction of seeing him fail.

He shook off Robin's arm. 'I'll be fine, Rob.'

'No, you're not,' Robin said, catching him as he stumbled. 'You're stubborn that's all. Denzil, he can't ride like this.'

'Ride you will, Adam, even if I have to tie you to the saddle,' Denzil replied. 'It will be dark in a few hours and I would like to close some miles between here and Oxford. Now on the horse.'

Adam surveyed the unprepossessing mount Robin had found. He had no choice it seemed. He set his mind to endure what would be a hellish few hours and, with Robin's help, managed to straddle the beast without falling off the other side. Winding his fingers into the animal's mane, he gritted his teeth and let it do the work.

Mercifully, the weather confounded Denzil's plans. The conditions worsened, dumping cold, soaking rain on the party. Soaked to the skin and so cold he couldn't contain his chattering teeth, Adam gave up the unequal struggle and slumped across his horse's neck, the harsh hair of the mane resting against his face. He sensed someone ride up beside him and felt a hand on his shoulder. From a distance he heard Robin's voice.

'Denzil, this is ridiculous. He can't go any further and it's gone dark. We're only a couple of miles from Preswood. Take him there. We can rest for the night.'

Denzil grunted and muttered something that sounded like agreement and Adam closed his eyes with relief.

Robin's fingers tightened on him, shaking him awake. 'Stay with us, Adam. We're nearly at Preswood.'

They're taking me to Perdita, he thought. Perdita, with her stillroom and her calm efficient manner that had saved the lives of the men he had brought to her after Edgehill. Perdita, whose slender body he had held in his arms on the ride back from Stratford. Perdita, whose brown eyes drifted unbidden into his dreams as they did even now.

Every step the horse took echoed her name. 'Perdita, Perdita, Perdita.'

Through the fog of semi consciousness, the horse came to halt. Denzil could be heard arguing with a woman, but at first he couldn't make out any words. The squabbling voices came closer and the woman said, 'How dare you presume on us like this, Denzil Marchant.'

Joan he thought, giving Denzil a scolding just as she did when he had been a boy. The memory made him smile.

'Perdita, thank heavens you are here,' Joan said. 'Denzil has a wounded man with him. See what needs to be done.'

A gentle hand touched his knee. 'Sir, where are you hurt?'

Adam raised his head and turned toward the voice, blinking in the light of the lantern she held up to his face.

'Perdita. I'm sorry to be a trouble.'

Her hand slipped from his knee and she took a step back. 'Adam.'

Joan's voice again, strident with fury. 'Adam? Your prisoner is Adam? And what pray do you intend to do with him?'

'He's going to Oxford to be tried as the traitor that he is,' Denzil boomed back at his aunt.

'If he lives,' Perdita said.

'Oh, I'm not going to die just yet,' Adam tried to say but he didn't think anyone heard him.

'Enough talk. We have to get him inside.' Robin touched his arm. 'Adam? This is going to hurt but there's no easy way to get you off this horse. Ludovic, help me here.'

Robin tugged at his belt and Adam slid sideways off the horse in a blinding dissonance of pain.

His brother's arm around his waist stopped him sliding to the ground.

'I can stand,' he muttered.

'Fine. Stand then.

Robin let go of him and as Adam's knees buckled, hauled him up again.

'I have him, sir.'

Before Adam could argue Ludovic had picked him up like a child and carried him across the forecourt and into the house.

Perdita trailed Ludovic into the house, ignoring the Marchant brothers. She had no time for the niceties of hospitality. Joan or Bess could take care of that.

Ludovic deposited Adam in a corner of the heavy oak settle in the Great Hall. Adam leaned his head back against the oak and closed his eyes as Perdita fumbled with the sodden cords of his cloak. His face felt like ice to her touch and she took his hands in hers, chafing them in a futile attempt to instill some warmth back into him.

His eyes flickered open and he raised his hand to touch her hair, which hung in damp cat's tails around her face.

'Perdita, you're soaked.'

She managed a tight smile. 'I'll dry but we need to get you out of these sodden clothes before you take lung fever. What was your brother thinking dragging a wounded man across the country in this weather?'

'I think he is trying to kill me,' Adam said and his eyes closed.

'How is he?' Joan hovered over her.

Perdita did not need to ask where Adam had been hurt. An orange sash, now died a watery red from blood, had been roughly tied around his left thigh. She looked up at Robin.

'Ball or sword?'

Robin flicked back his rain darkened hair and frowned. 'Pistol ball. I think it's still in there,' Robin replied.

Denzil's shadow loomed behind her and he boomed in her ear, 'Well, Mistress Gray? How long will it take to patch him up so he's fit to ride?'

She rose to her feet and faced Denzil, the rage only just below the surface. 'What were you thinking forcing a man with a leg wound to ride any distance in this rain? You will be lucky if the wound doesn't kill him, then lung fever will. I need to get him to a bed and tend the wound properly.'

Denzil shrugged. 'Do what you must. We'll be gone in the morning and you need trouble yourself no more.'

'If your brother lives the night.' Perdita responded.

She turned to the sea of concerned faces surrounding her, seeking out the one she needed.

'Ludovic, can you get Captain Coulter to the guest chamber?'

As Ludovic saw to Adam, Perdita went in search of the things she needed and by the time she joined Ludovic in the guest chamber, he had stripped Adam of his soaking clothes and boots, which lay in a sodden heap on the floor.

Perdita laid the basket of bandages and remedies she had gleaned from the stillroom on the table and crossed to the still figure on the bed. Ludovic had pulled a blanket over the naked man and turned to the fire, stoking it high and setting a pot to boil his instruments.

Perdita sat on the edge of the bed and surveyed her patient. Adam's eyes were closed, his breathing shallow and ragged.

She turned the blanket aside to look at the wound. She had never really seen a man naked before. Samuel had always come to her bed in a nightgown, just raising it sufficiently to do what he had to do, his corpulent body hot and heavy on hers. Perdita shuddered at the memory of the nightly assault she had endured until a child had been conceived, and when she had lost the child she carried, a result of a 'chastisement' as Samuel had called it, he had returned, desperate for a son. Even now the bile rose in her throat.

By contrast the body beneath her hands was lean and well-muscled. The brown of his face ended abruptly at his collar line, forming a contrast to the lighter skin of his body. A smattering of dark hair curled on his chest and crept down his taut flat stomach toward his groin. Perdita took a breath, wondering for a moment what it would be like to be held against this hard, strong body. A vague memory of the ride back from Stratford crept unbidden into her memory—a scent of man and horse and a broad chest on which to lay her head...

She picked up his hand and turned it over, noting the scars and callouses that spoke of a hard life. Even by the light of the candles, visible beneath the tan of his wrist were other scars, lighter marks in the weather darkened skin.

She looked up to find Ludovic watching her.

'Manacles,' he said, pushing back his own cuff to show her

similar scars. 'He's been a captive somewhere in his past. To work, Mistress Gray.'

Perdita gently eased the rough pad away from the wound and flinched as it started to bleed again.

Ludovic wiped the blood away and peered closer at the small neat hole which marked the pistol ball's entrance. 'I've seen worse, but there is no exit would so we must get the ball out, if it is not too deep.'

Perdita swallowed. She had also seen worse but it was easier to be dispassionate about a stranger, not a man she considered a friend. A friend? She pushed that uncertainty to the back of her mind as Adam moved beneath her hands and groaned.

'Sorry to be such a confounded nuisance,' he murmured.

'How did this happen?' she asked, more to distract him then out of curiosity.

'Denzil ambushed my convoy.'

He grimaced as Ludovic began to clean around the wound, his hand seeking Perdita's. The bones of her hand crunched as he grasped it tightly, hissing between his teeth.

'Curse Denzil.'

'Denzil?'

'It's his pistol ball,' Adam grunted.

Perdita stared at him. 'Your own brother shot you? Did he know it was you?'

Adam swallowed. 'I prefer to give him the benefit of the doubt. Are you done yet, Ludovic? It feels like you're taking my leg off.'

'I haven't even started yet,' Ludovic replied. He glanced up at Perdita. 'We need help, Mistress Gray. If he's conscious, he will need to be held down. Perhaps Master Robin?'

'Rob's done enough for one day. Just do what you must do, Ludovic,' Adam muttered, 'I'll behave.'

Ludovic put a hand on his shoulder. 'It will hurt.'

'It hurts now. Just be quick about it.'

Ludovic took a roll of leather from his bag and pushed it between Adam's teeth. 'Now keep still,' he ordered and began his work with brisk efficiency, producing the flattened lead projectile with a bloody flourish as Adam fell back on the bolsters in a faint.

As Ludovic tied the last of the bandages, he glanced across at Perdita who flexed her fingers with a grimace. 'Is your hand all right, mistress?' Ludovic asked.

'It will be. What about Adam, will he be all right?' Perdita asked.

Ludovic glanced at his patient and shrugged. 'The wound itself is not so bad and he is strong enough to fight it. There is a strong risk of lung fever after that ride in the rain and if Lord Marchant is to insist on moving him tomorrow.' He glanced toward the door at the sound of raised voices coming closer.

The door flung open and Denzil stood glaring at them. Behind him Perdita could make out the pale and determined face of his aunt.

'Are you done, Mistress Gray?' Denzil roared, addressing Perdita who quailed as he turned the full force of his rage on her. 'If so I will take my prisoner and leave you. Robin? Where are you, dammit?'

Robin pushed past his brother, placing himself between Denzil and the bed. 'No. He stays where he is, Denzil.'

A vein throbbed in Denzil's temple. 'I'll not stay in this house to be lectured to by women.' Denzil cast his aunt a fiery glance.

Perdita moved beside Robin, casting him a quick, nervous glance as she said, 'You can't take him. He'll die if you move him.'

'Pah.' Denzil took a step toward her. 'Adam is tough and if it's rest he needs he will get ample in Oxford Castle.'

'Haven't you done enough already? He's lost blood and has the risk of a fever. Move him and you'll kill him.'

'Well, that will save us all a lot of trouble.' Denzil pushed past

Perdita and in a couple of strides he crossed to the bed and leaned over Adam. 'Can you hear me, Coulter?'

Adam's eyes flickered open. 'Denzil.' His voice was barely above a whisper.

'Don't make yourself comfortable, brother. You're coming to Oxford to stand trial for the traitor that you are.'

'For the love of God, Denzil, you've shot me, beaten me and dragged me through the rain. I can't sit up, let alone sit a horse,' Adam said.

'You'll come with me, even if it means throwing you in the back of a dung cart to get you there.' Denzil gripped the bed clothes. 'Now get up.'

Perdita laid her hand on his sleeve, her fury with this obdurate man seething to the surface.

'You'll not take him.'

Denzil shook off her hand, turning his ferocious gaze on her. He raised his hand. Instinctively she took a quick inward breath, bracing herself for the blow, knowing from bitter experience what was coming.

'Denzil. Strike her and you'll reckon with me,' Adam pulled himself up in the bed, his face pale and his eyes burning.

Denzil lowered his hand and laughed. 'And what will you do, Adam?'

Adam closed his eyes. 'Perdita, would you be so good as to find me some dry clothes?'

Robin took his brother's arm and steered him away from the bed. 'Apart from the fact it is still pouring with rain, Denzil, it is the middle of the night and I for one would like something to eat and a dry bed. Mistress Gray is right, Adam will die if you try to move him. Look at him. You can see for yourself, he'll not be fit for any sort of travel for days, if not weeks.'

Denzil glared at his younger brother and back at the man on

the bed. Adam's gaze held his brother's for a moment before he slumped back against the bolsters.

'Denzil, I give you my parole,' Adam said.

'Your parole? Do you think your word means anything to me?' Denzil snarled.

'Then leave me here, Denzil. I'll bring him on to Oxford when he can sit a horse,' Robin said in a low even tone.

Denzil scrutinised his youngest brother through narrowed eyes.

'You don't trust me?' Robin met his brother's gaze, his face pale and taut, and it occurred to Perdita in that moment that if there was one person in the world who could control Denzil Marchant, it was this slight young man.

Denzil shook his head and clapped a hand on his brother's shoulder. 'Of course I trust you. It's him I don't trust.' Denzil glared in Adam's direction and gave an impatient snort. 'Very well, Coulter, it seems if I want you hale and hearty to stand trial for the traitor you are, I have no choice but to accept your parole and leave you in Robin's custody.' Robin's shoulders visibly relaxed but stiffened again as Denzil rounded on him. 'If you let him escape, Rob, then God help you.'

'Leave the boy alone.' Adam's voice was cold and hard. 'I've given you my word Denzil. That should be enough.'

Denzil's moustache twitched as he turned back to Adam, leaning over him so close that his hair brushed Adam's face. 'Don't go and die on me, Coulter, it would be very disappointing.'

'I don't doubt it.' Adam glared back at him.

Denzil turned on his heel and strode out of the room.

Robin crossed to Perdita and laid his hand on her shoulder. Now the drama had passed and with it the realisation of what facing down a man like Denzil Marchant meant, she began to shake.

'I've never seen anyone stand up to Denzil like that,' Robin said, unable to hide the admiration in his tone.

She looked up at him and said between clenched teeth. 'You did well yourself.'

Joan, who had remained silent during the exchange sank on to a chair by the fire and rested her forehead on her hand.

'It is as if the clock has been turned back twenty years,' she said. 'Denzil and Adam. Always Denzil and Adam.'

Robin crossed to the bed and looked down at his brother. 'You look convincingly terrible,' he said.

Adam gave a snort of laughter, his hand flying to his ribs. 'I've felt better. Thank you, Robin. You didn't need to take my part.'

Robin shrugged. 'I'm sorry it has come to this, Adam.'

Adam frowned. 'Sorry for what? My quarrel is with Denzil and Louise, never with you. Whatever our political differences, at least let us put our filial differences to one side. I gave Denzil my parole and you have my word I'll not break it. Go and leave me to sleep, for God's sake. We'll talk tomorrow.'

'Tomorrow,' Robin said and glanced at the shuttered window. 'I think it's already tomorrow. God's death, I crave a bed.'

Perdita stood aside to let Robin pass, telling him to seek out some food in the kitchens and she would see that a bed was prepared for him in one of the spare chambers.

Joan rose to her feet as the sound of Robin's boots sounded on the stairs. She crossed to the bed and picked up Adam's hand, pressing it to her lips.

'I'm sorry to bring such strife to this house,' Adam murmured.

'Don't fool yourself that Robin's noble offer has anything to do with you,' Joan said. 'I'm quite sure that the longer you are indisposed, the happier Robin will be.'

'What do you mean?'

Perdita smiled and caught Joan's eye. 'It seems that Robin and Bess have formed an attachment,' she replied.

'Ah,' Adam said. 'A woman. Always a woman.'

Perdita reached out to smooth the bolsters but Adam put a restraining hand on hers.

'Don't fuss Perdita. If I need anyone I'll call for Ludovic.'

Perdita collected the sodden clothes and at the door turned back to glance at the bed. His eyes were closed and apparently unaware that Perdita watched her, Joan smoothed the hair away from his forehead in a maternal gesture. Left with the strange sensation of having seen something that was not hers to see, Perdita closed the door and crept away.

Chapter Eight

PRESWOOD HALL, JUNE 1643

'W hat are you reading?' Robin asked.
Adam rolled over and hauled himself painfully up on
the bolsters. He held up the battered leather-bound volume.

'Joan lent me Geoffrey Clifford's journal of his travels,' he said.
'I wish that I'd been able to visit even half the places Geoffrey did
in his wanderings.'

Robin took the book from him and flicked through the pages.
'You spent six years on the Continent; you must have tales of your
own to tell.'

Adam's mouth twisted into a rueful smile. 'Several of those
years were spent in Leipzig Castle. Anyway, I had no money for the
indulgence of travel, Rob. I had to earn my living the only way I
knew how, with my sword. What brings you up here?'

Robin shrugged and a rueful smile curled the corners of his
mouth. 'A need to escape the company of women for a while, no
matter how delightful that company might be. Do you play cards?'

'Of course. You know the rules of Penneech?'

Robin nodded. He pulled up a chair beside the bed and dealt the cards.

'How's the leg?'

'I can't put any weight on it yet, but it's the damned ribs that hurt the most. Just don't make me laugh.'

Robin looked up. 'Now there's a challenge.'

'Speaking of the delightful company of women, do I gather it is in your interest to prolong my convalescence?' Adam asked without meeting his brother's eyes.

'What do you mean?'

Adam looked up and caught the flush rising in Robin's face. 'A certain Elizabeth Clifford?'

Robin straightened his shoulders as if to deny the charge and then relaxed with a crooked smile. 'Aye, there's no doubt I fancy myself in love with the girl.'

They played in silence for a couple of minutes before Robin asked. 'Have you ever been in love?'

Adam paused, apparently considering his hand. 'I imagined myself in love once, but it was lust not love.'

'Louise?' Robin suggested.

'Yes, Louise,' Adam said with a heavy sigh. 'Since then there have been women but no time for love.'

'What really happened that night?'

Robin's casual tone could not hide the curiosity that had probably plagued him all these years. He deserved the truth.

Adam closed his eyes. 'I was your age, Rob and, gull that I was, fell for Louise the day that she and Denzil were betrothed. I worshipped her and she gave me every encouragement. When she summoned me to her bedchamber I went like an eager puppy, and there she was waiting for me, dressed only in a nightshift looking like a goddess.'

Robin snorted with bitter laughter. 'I can imagine.'

'Well you can also imagine what my thoughts were. My seduction had begun. She offered me wine and blandishments. I had stripped down to my breeches and was lying beside her on the bed when her brother burst in with sword drawn.' Adam took a breath. 'I had no alternative but to defend myself and I was ever the better swordsman than Philip. He ran on my sword. Louise started screaming rape and murder. She ripped her shift and scratched her own face. The rest you know.'

Robin sighed. 'Father was summoned to deal with the mess?'

Adam closed his eyes. 'He wouldn't even hear my side of the story. All he saw was a beautiful woman claiming I had raped her, her brother dying in her arms. He told me I was to leave the country that night if a scandal was to be avoided and I did. I left, and by leaving confirmed my guilt.'

'You were not the first, nor shall you be the last. Poor Denzil paid a heavy penance by marrying Louise,' Robin observed.

Adam's mouth twitched. 'He went willingly, Robin.'

'He did,' Robin conceded. 'And I think he still imagines he's in love with her.'

'They've no children?'

Robin shrugged. 'No child of the marriage, but I know Denzil has at least one by-blow, so the fault must rest with Louise.'

Adam flinched. 'Does he acknowledge the child?'

Robin looked up from his cards. 'I'm sorry, Adam, I forgot.'

Adam shrugged. 'It's no matter, Robin.'

'The child and the mother are well provided for, I believe.'

'My one regret,' Adam said, 'is that I never had a chance to make my peace with our father before he died.'

Robin appeared to be considering his hand of cards. 'I think,' he said slowly, 'that once Louise's nature became better known, father may have been more inclined to forgive you, but then we got the news that you were dead.'

The breath stopped in Adam's throat. 'He thought I was dead?'

'Aye, we had word that you had fallen at,' Robin frowned, 'was it Vlotho?'

'I was wounded and taken prisoner but I had no means to send word that I was alive. If you can call it that, but my captors told me they had sent word of my capture and were demanding a ransom so father must have known I still lived.'

Robin stared at him. 'Maybe father was never told. Maybe the word came to Denzil first.' He glanced away. 'Maybe that was why the ransom was never paid.'

The cold, grey walls of Leipzig closed in on Adam once more. That made sense. Denzil had known his circumstances but chose neither to tell his father nor pay the ransom demanded for his release. Denzil had wanted him to die in the dungeons of Leipzig, forgotten and unmourned.

'He must hate me very much,' Adam said.

Robin shook his head. 'No. It is Louise who would have had the last word. But if no ransom was paid, how were you released?'

Adam shook his head. 'They must have wearied of me. I found myself cast out on to the streets with only the rags on my back in the middle of winter.'

Robin stared at him. 'Then how did you get back to England?'

Adam turned his attention back to his cards. 'That is a story for another time, Rob. Your move, I believe.'

He waited until Robin had played his cards and then said without looking up. 'Did Father—did he—say anything when he heard of my death?'

'No, but he shut himself in the library for days. When he did come out, he said, "He was the best of you." and that was the last time you were ever mentioned in the house.'

Adam looked down at his hand and saw that it was shaking.

Perdita laid the paper and pens down on the table in front of Adam. 'There you are, as requested.'

Adam picked up one of the pens and pulled a piece of paper in front of him.

'If Denzil hears you're on your feet...' she began.

'Who's going to tell him? Robin? It suits Robin fine to have me incapacitated as long as he can. Trust me, Perdita, I have no intention of ending up in Oxford Castle.'

'But you've given your parole.'

Adam smiled, a thin-lipped smile. 'And I have every intention of honouring it. There are other ways to get myself out of this bind.'

Perdita sat down beside the window with her sewing as he wrote his letter. She watched as he filled the page with a neat, orderly hand, poured the red wax to seal it and imprinted his seal from a ring on his right hand. He sat toying with the letter, staring past Perdita to the world beyond the window.

He set the letter down and picked up his pen again, his hand straying toward the sheets of papers. Almost unconsciously a few lines began to appear under his hand.

'What are you doing?' Perdita asked.

'Please don't move, Perdita. The light from the window is framing your face and I cannot let the moment pass. Permit me.'

She blinked. 'You can draw?'

'Did you think Joan the only one in the family with a talent for art?' Adam's mouth twitched into a smile. 'Although Joan has more talent in her small finger than I possess in total and I would not compare myself to her. I just find faces interest me. It proved a useful skill in Leipzig. Stay still. It won't take long.'

He smoothed out a fresh piece of paper and sharpened the pen.

'Am I permitted to talk?' Perdita asked.

'If you don't move too much.'

'How was it useful in Leipzig?' she asked.

'I took small commissions. I did likenesses of the guards, their wives, their children, and I was paid with favours. It kept me alive. It also gave me the pennies I needed to make my way back to England.'

'Why do you find my face interesting?' she asked.

'I find all faces interesting. I can learn all I need about a person by looking in their eyes and the turn of their mouth.'

He fixed her with a steady gaze as if studying every inch of her face and the line of her head. Perdita watched his hand moving across the paper with the long -practiced skill.

'You had no children with your husband?' he asked.

Perdita started at the unexpected question. 'No... none that lived.' She caught at the material in her skirt, pleating it between her fingers, willing the old pain to go away. 'I have no wish to talk about my marriage or the children that might have been. I left all that behind me in London.'

His hand had stopped and he studied her face with such disconcerting intensity that she had to look away and she said aloud the words that crowded her mind. 'I've learned to live with the pain of that lost child, but it's there, every day of my life.'

'There will be other children,' Adam said.

She turned to look at him, the pain jagged in her throat as she blurted out, 'But there will always be that little ghost at my skirt.'

For a very long moment, neither of them moved. They stared at each other transfixed by the raw emotion that lay between them.

Perdita broke the eye contact and took a deep breath. 'You're right, though. God willing, there will be children when I wed Simon.'

He turned his attention back to the drawing. 'When will that be?'

'Christmas,' she said. 'We have decided that as soon as the

campaigning ends for this year, we will be wed. Poor Simon had been so sure it would not come this far, but there we are.'

Adam set the pen down and leaned back scrutinising his work. 'It is done. Just a quick sketch.'

'Can I see?' Perdita rose to her feet and Adam handed her the paper.

As she looked down at her image, a rush of conflicting emotions overcame her. She saw the same face that stared back at her each day from the mirror, but her life story was drawn in the line of the jaw and the set of her eyes. It was as if he had looked into her very soul and seen the pain of the loss of her child, the nightmare of her marriage, her loneliness and something else... something deep and frightening that involved this man.

'Do I really look like that?' she said with a forced laugh

'No, Perdita, you are much more beautiful.'

She raised her gaze to meet his eyes. No man had ever told her she was beautiful or looked at her in the way he looked at her now. She saw desire and tenderness, more profound than the simple adoration she saw in Simon's eyes, reflected in the eyes of this stranger. In an instant, his face closed over. He took the paper from her, screwed it up and flung it into the fireplace where a small fire burned against the unseasonable chill.

'Why did you do that?' she asked.

'It was not very good,' he said quickly.

'Perdita. You are needed in the kitchen.' Bess poked her head around the door. 'There you are. Cook has burned the chicken and there is a frightful row. Can you deal with him? I fear I shall have a saucepan thrown at me. How are you today, Captain Coulter?'

'I am well enough, Mistress Clifford. Could I ask a favour of you?'

'Of course,' Bess replied.

'Can you ask Robin to come to me?'

After Bess tripped off in search of Robin, Adam hauled himself out of the chair and limped painfully to the fireplace. The drawing he had made of Perdita had fallen just short of the smouldering embers and he bent to retrieve it. He smoothed the creases, folded it and barely had time to put it inside his jacket before Robin entered without knocking.

'You sent for me?' Robin gave his brother a sarcastic bow.

'I have a favour to ask of you,' Adam said.

Robin's eyes narrowed. 'What?'

'I would be grateful if you could deliver this.'

Robin took the letter Adam held out for him. He read the name and looked up at Adam his eyes wide with surprise. 'This is addressed to—'

'I know to whom it is addressed,' Adam cut across his brother. 'He knows you, Robin. You can give it into his hand.'

Robin waved the missive. 'I believe he is with the queen. She landed in Yorkshire some weeks ago and is on her way south to Oxford.'

Adam took a sharp intake of breath. 'The queen? Are you certain? That means Louise is back in the country.' As soon as Louise had Denzil's ear, he would be a dead man. 'Even more reason to see this letter delivered, Rob.'

'But I'm supposed to be guarding you,' Robin pointed out. 'I can't do that if I'm gallivanting off around the countryside, delivering your mail.'

'Robin.' Adam smiled and held out his hands. 'Look at me, I can barely walk, let alone make a bid for freedom. I gave Denzil my parole and I intend to honour it.'

Robin raised a quizzical eyebrow. 'Very well, I'll do this boon for you, but you better be here when I get back.'

'I will be. Thank you, Rob.'

From his window, Adam leaned against the casement and watched Robin ride away. He jerked around as the door opened with a faint click and Joan entered, carrying a leather folio and a pile of clothes, which she set down on the chest.

'I thought you would prefer your own clothes,' she said. 'Robin's taste is somewhat more flamboyant than yours.'

Adam plucked at the slashed sleeves and gilt lace of the blue jacket he wore. 'Not quite.'

He took off the borrowed jacket, replaced it with his own serviceable uniform jacket and limped back to his chair, easing his leg back on to the stool. Behind him, Joan folded the discarded jacket and laid it on the bed. When she was done, she joined him, setting out some sketches from the folio on the table.

'I want to know what you think of these,' she said. 'I intend the painting as a wedding present for Simon and Perdita.'

Adam picked up the preliminary sketches of a man and woman. Even drawn roughly in charcoal he could see without hesitation that she had drawn Simon Clifford standing behind a seated Perdita, his hand resting on her shoulder. A traditional pose but his heart clenched at the proprietary gesture. Perdita Gray would be Perdita Clifford by the end of the year.

'You do have a wonderful talent,' he said.

'So do you,' Joan said.

He looked up at the sharp edge to her tone. 'What do you mean?'

Joan considered her drawing for a long moment, her finger resting on the still representation of Perdita. 'I have no trouble in capturing Simon but Perdita has an elusive quality.' Joan held out a folded, creased paper and spread it before him. 'I found this in Robin's jacket just now. This is your work?'

Adam looked down at the sketch he had done of Perdita. He

had forgotten to retrieve it before he changed his jacket. His breath caught and he said between tight lips. 'I was just—'

'Adam, this is how Perdita should look for the man she loves and that man is not Simon.'

Adam crumpled the paper in his hand but he refrained from tossing it into the fireplace again. 'What is the point in lying to you Joan when you know me so well?'

She cocked her head to one side, her mouth drooping as she laid her hand over his.

'Is it your fate to always fall for women who belong to other men?'

He gave a bitter laugh, 'Apparently it is.'

'Does she know how you feel?'

Adam met his aunt's eyes, horrified at the thought. 'I hope not.'

'What are you going to do?'

He extricated his hand from hers and shrugged. 'Do? What can I do? I have nothing to offer her. Simon Clifford is a good man and he deserves her and she him. I genuinely wish them both happiness.'

Joan brushed a tear from her eye and he leaned forward taking her hands in his.

'It is my intention to be gone from here within days and, God willing, Perdita will marry her Simon at Christmas without further thought of me. There is no more to be said on the subject.'

A relapse of fever kept Adam to his bed for the next couple of days with Ludovic in attendance. Not wishing a repeat of their last, troubling conversation, Perdita busied herself with other domestic duties.

The summer weather continued foul and rain lashed the

windows, bowing the trees and masking the arrival of a large body of mounted men until they were almost upon the house. The sound of bellowed orders and the whinnying of horses brought Perdita running from the parlour where she had been mending sheets. She narrowly avoided a collision with Joan, coming out of Adam's bed chamber.

Joan caught her arm. 'Don't run, Perdita. We are not being invaded. Adam says he is expecting Prince Rupert,' her hand flew to her throat. 'The prince himself, here at Preswood!'

Before Perdita could ask how Adam knew the king's nephew, he had arrived on their doorstep, the great hall below them reverberating with male voices and heavy cavalry boots.

'This way, your Highness.' Robin's voice could be heard above the general hub bub.

Perdita peered over the bannister. A tall, dark haired, startlingly handsome young man stood framed by the great front doorway, his broad shoulders nearly spanning the width of the entrance. He scanned the room with hooded eyes while he removed his gloves and shook the soaked cloak from his shoulders.

Joan made a shooing gesture. 'Go and greet him.'

Cursing her choice of the oldest and most worn gown she owned, Perdita hurried down the stairs to where Bess had already taken charge of the situation, sinking into a deep curtsey before the Prince, apparently untroubled by the sudden appearance of a prince and thirty hungry young men.

'Your Highness, you are most welcome to Preswood. I trust you will be staying for some refreshment?' Bess said.

He acknowledged her with a peremptory bow, his dark eyes sweeping across Bess from her foot to the top of her head. Apparently approving of what he saw, his dark face broke into a broad grin.

'Thank you, Mistress Clifford.' His voice betrayed only the slightest hint of an accent. 'My men and I would be grateful for your hospitality, but I do not intend to intrude on you for long. My business is with one Adam Coulter. Is he here?'

Perdita and Bess exchanged quick questioning glances. 'Captain Coulter is upstairs,' Bess said. 'He is recovering from a recent wound.'

'Take me to him.'

Perdita stepped forward. 'If you would care to come with me, your Highness.'

With Robin following, the prince took the stairs two at a time, bursting in through the open door to Adam's bedchamber without ceremony.

'Well, Coulter?' he boomed.

Adam rose to his feet and inclined his head. 'Your Highness. It is a great pleasure to see you again.'

Robin made a sound that seemed halfway between a laugh and a stifled choke.

Rupert turned to him with a smile. 'You are surprised, Marchant? I told you, your brother and I are old comrades-in-arms. Are we not, Coulter?' He strode across to Adam and clapped him on the shoulder with a force that caused Adam to wince.

Adam rubbed his ribs and managed a crooked smile. 'Indeed, your highness.'

Adam was a tall man but Prince Rupert overtopped him by at least six inches.

Rupert glanced around the room and strolled over to the table where Adam and Joan had been playing chess. He picked up the king and inspected it. 'I owe a debt to Adam Coulter and one which I am now able to repay.'

Those dark eyes did not miss the quick glance that passed between Perdita and Robin, and Rupert set the chess piece back.

'Ah. You're wondering, perhaps, what debt it is I owe this man who wears the colours of my uncle's enemy?'

'I am curious,' Robin said.

'Some years ago, we fought together to try to regain my broth-er's throne. A bold time was it not?' He directed this enquiry at Adam, who nodded agreement. 'Until Vlotho.' The prince's face darkened.

'Indeed, your Highness. Until Vlotho,' Adam echoed.

Rupert smiled. 'I was eighteen. The blood ran hotter than it does now.'

From what Perdita knew of this young giant's reputation at twenty-five, it must have been positively volcanic at eighteen.

'I would have died rather than surrender. I recall I was surrounded. My enemies demanded to know who I was. I would not tell them. I just declared my rank... '

'And they responded "*Mein Gott*, if you are a Colonel, you are a very young one".' Adam's laugh cut short, his hand flying to his sore ribs.

Rupert smiled. 'I would have been killed,' he said, 'had it not been for the intervention of my friend here who informed them who I was in no uncertain terms and took a musket butt on the skull for his pains.' He looked at Adam with narrowed eyes. 'You know, Coulter, there were many times in Leipzig when I wondered about the nature of the debt I owed you for my life. Sometimes death seemed preferable.' He shrugged. 'But as uncomfortable as my confinement may have been, I imagine I had it easier than you.'

The two men looked at each other with the deep under-standing of men who have shared a common suffering. Perdita wondered how it would have been for a young man such as Rupert to have endured such close confinement at a time when he should have been enjoying the full fruits of his youth. If it had been hard for Adam it must have been hell on earth for Rupert.

Rupert clapped Adam on the shoulder again with a force that made Adam stagger.

'Well, come my friend. We must talk. You,' Rupert snapped his fingers at Perdita, 'perhaps you will bring me some lunch. I could eat a horse.'

Rupert of the Rhine, as he was known by all, flung himself down on a chair at the table, waiting while Adam resumed his own seat.

'So, Coulter, you have got yourself in a little trouble,' Rupert said.

'It would seem so.'

'I have heard the stories. That business with your brother. Zounds, Coulter, what were you thinking when you swived Marchant's wife?'

Adam shrugged. 'My thoughts, if I had any, were those of any young man when presented with a willing and beautiful woman.' *And I never actually got to do any swiving*, he almost added. Instead he shrugged. 'It was seven years ago and I'm not the same person. Leipzig saw to that.'

'Well, the lady hasn't forgotten you.' Rupert picked up another of the chess pieces, the queen. 'She is lovely that lady, but dangerous.' He glanced up at Adam with a rueful smile. 'I doubt I would have done much different, but that doesn't explain why, in God's name, you have taken up arms against my uncle?' The chess piece fell back on to the board and Rupert's fierce gaze met Adam's, challenging the old loyalty they had to each other. The loyalty Adam had betrayed.

Adam took a breath. He didn't need to antagonise Rupert, not now when he needed his help. 'Because I don't believe that your uncle can rule without the consent of the people. His decision to do so has inflicted suffering and misery on his people in untold measure.'

'You think you know him?' Rupert's eyes narrowed in challenge.

'I think he doesn't understand his countrymen,' Adam said carefully.

'Coulter, the king will win this war and where will that leave you?'

Adam shrugged. 'Much the same place I am now, I suspect.'

Rupert threw himself back in the chair and regarded him, his finger resting on his unshaven upper lip. 'You would not consider joining me? I need men of your calibre and experience.'

Adam thought carefully before replying. 'Your Highness, I hold you in the highest regard but I cannot turn my coat. I fight for what I believe in, not for the honour or the glory or indeed, in this matter, the money.'

Rupert shrugged. 'A man must live with his conscience, and I will respect you for that, but I am saddened that we must find each other in opposite camps.'

'And I, your Highness,' Adam said with genuine feeling. Once, a long time ago, he would have followed Rupert into the pits of hell.

Rupert spread his hands. 'Here and now, we are at truce. Old friends and comrades. What is it that you wish me to do?'

Before Adam could answer there was a gentle knock at the door and Perdita entered bearing a tray.

'Zounds, that smells good.' Rupert looked appreciatively at the tray laden with pasties and fruit.

His gaze ran equally appreciatively up and down Perdita and a protective pang jolted Adam. No man had the right to look at Perdita in such a way, prince or not.

'Your Highness, may I present Mistress Gray.'

Perdita curtsied.

'Mistress Gray is a most able nurse, your Highness. I believe I owe her my life.'

Rupert raised an eyebrow. 'Ah well, I would that when I am so unfortunate as to be wounded in battle that I may have so attractive a nurse.' He smiled. 'Thank you, Mistress Gray.'

Recognising she had been dismissed, Perdita shot Adam a quick, questioning glance, before leaving the room.

Rupert devoured one of the pasties in a couple of mouthfuls. 'A most attractive woman, Coulter,' he said as he reached for a second.

'Another man's wife, or soon to be.'

Rupert raised a questioning eyebrow as pastry crumbs fell to the table in a shower. 'Who is the fortunate man?' he asked with his mouth full.

'Simon Clifford. This is his house.'

Rupert brushed the crumbs from his jacket. 'Ah yes. I have met the man. One of Northampton's officer. Not a soldier.' Rupert regarded him for a long moment. 'To business. So your brother wants to see you hanged?'

'Apparently.'

He waited while Rupert quaffed the jack of ale. He set it down as he wiped his mouth. 'Surely my uncle would not concern himself with a mere captain of horse?'

'I do not need to tell you that my brother's wife has some powerful friends among the king's advisors. I have no doubt they would see my death warrant signed for the chance of a few nights in bed with her.'

A smile lit Rupert's dark features and he laughed, throwing back his head. 'Ah, Coulter,' he said. 'I would probably arrange it myself for that pleasure.' The smile faded. 'Now, what is it you think I can do?'

'Release me from my parole.'

Rupert stared at him thoughtfully. 'That is a big thing you ask of me.'

'I wouldn't ask it unless I knew it was within your power, your Highness.'

Rupert's eyes narrowed. 'Well I have already given you one option. You won't reconsider and join with me?'

Adam met his former commander's gaze. It would be so easy to say yes and join Rupert once more, but what was at stake here was greater than the fate of a small German palatinate. He fought for his country, for his beliefs.

'No, your Highness. My word is given.'

'So be it.' The prince brushed the last of the crumbs from his clothes, stood up and strode to the door in two strides. He stopped and turned once more. 'Your brother is with the queen, only a day's ride from Stratford. I plan to meet them there tomorrow. If I encounter him, I will intervene directly with him and tell him that you are a free man.'

'Thank you, your Highness.'

Rupert shrugged. 'In case I am distracted. Have you paper? I will sign a pass for you.' He scrawled a few lines and signed it with a flourish, sealing the document with his own ring. He folded it and handed it to Adam. 'I would advise you to depart this place as soon as possible. I cannot answer for your brother's next actions.'

'Thank you, your Highness.' Adam rose to his feet and inclined his head.

At the door, Rupert glanced back. 'The debt is paid, Coulter. If it is our misfortune to meet on the field of battle, there will be no quarter.'

'And none expected.'

The door slammed shut behind Rupert and within ten minutes all was quiet. Adam leaned against the window casement watching the prince and his companions ride away. He blew out a breath. He had forgotten that the Prince could be an exhausting companion.

Robin peered around the door, anger tempered with confusion on his face.

'Why didn't tell me you knew the prince?' he demanded as Adam gestured for him to enter.

Adam limped back to the table and handed his brother Rupert's safe pass. 'I didn't want Denzil removing me to some godforsaken part of the country if he knew that I was not entirely without friends in influential places.'

Robin broke the seal, scanned the paper and paled. 'Denzil will have apoplexy, and as for Louise, there will be hell to pay for this. Why didn't you tell me this was what you planned.'

'Because you wouldn't have gone.' Adam sank into his chair and ran a hand across his eyes. 'I'm sorry, Rob. I've probably brought a world of trouble down on your head.'

Robin met his eyes. 'I can manage Denzil,' he said, 'but Louise...' He shuddered and threw the paper back on the table. 'I do know one thing. You need to get back to Warwick as soon as you can before Denzil finds out that Rupert has released you from your parole.'

'I know.' Adam glanced at the window where rain lashed the diamond panes. 'If I leave now I can probably make Warwick by nightfall.'

Robin shook his head. 'I'm not going to try and dissuade you,' he said. 'I'll see what can be done about a horse.'

Perdita tied the knot on the bandage. 'Try that,' she said.

Adam tentatively rose to his feet, taking his weight on the bad leg that Perdita had padded and bound as firmly as she could.

'It will do,' he lied.

Perdita rose from her knees and crossed to the window where the rain still lashed unabated. 'You can't leave in this weather. You will be back in your sick bed.'

'I appreciate your concern.' Adam joined her at the window. His hand rested on her shoulder. 'I've no choice. I have to go now or Denzil and Louise will have my neck in a noose before the week's end.'

He was so close his breath lifted her hair. His fingers tightened on her shoulder, drawing her around to look up at him.

'Perdita,' he whispered.

She shivered. 'Adam, I...'

He laid a finger on her lips. 'Just let me look at you. I may never see you again.'

A cry of anguish stopped in her throat. *Never to see him again?*

'No.' she murmured. 'We will meet again. We must...' She leaned in toward him, willing him to hold her closer, to kiss her, but he drew back, swinging around to face the window at the sound of hoof beats.

'Damn it!' Adam cursed.

A knot of horsemen, wearing the Marchant colours rounded the bend in the drive with Denzil at their head. A woman in a scarlet riding costume, the matching feather in her hat, bedraggled and trailing down her back, rode beside him on a grey mare.

'Who is the woman?' Perdita asked, already knowing the answer.

'Louise,' Adam said, the name escaping on a breath.

Perdita turned to him and laid her hand on his chest, pushing him toward the door. 'Go now, Adam. Robin has a horse for you. I'll delay them.'

He shook his head, slamming his fist into the window sill. 'I couldn't go fast enough. However long you could delay them, I wouldn't reach Warwick.'

Perdita balled her hand and pounded his chest in impotent despair. 'Adam, you will lose everything if you stay. Denzil won't let you go, no matter how many passes the prince may write.'

He curled his hand around her neck and drew her close, resting his chin on the top of her head. 'Hush Perdita, this is not your concern.'

'But it is,' she said. 'You are my concern...'

This time, her words were silenced by his lips on hers, nothing more than a quick brush as he disengaged her, holding her at arm's length.

'Please don't fret on my account, Perdita. I am quite capable of looking after myself. Trust me.' He gently pushed her away. 'Go and greet your unexpected guests and hold them off as long as you can.' He glanced at the bed. 'I feel a sudden relapse coming on.'

Something like a smile twitched the corner of his mouth and Perdita nodded. She understood what needed to be done.

Taking a deep breath, she straightened her collar and cuffs and prepared for battle.

Chapter Nine

PRESWOOD HALL, JULY 2 1643

Louise Marchant swept into the Great Hall trailing Denzil in her wake. Despite being muddy and bedraggled from a long ride in the rain, Louise resembled an exotic bird that had found itself in the company of sparrows. Her sharp gaze raked the furnishings and the small group gathered at the foot of the stairs, barring access to the upper floors of the house.

'Joan.' With a smile on her lips that was not reflected in her eyes, Louise advanced on her husband's aunt. She bent and kissed Joan's cheek. 'How thin are! Nothing but skin and bone and... black. Joan, it does nothing for you.'

'It is an unexpected pleasure to see you too, Louise,' Joan responded in a glacial tone. 'May I introduce my stepdaughter, Elizabeth Clifford.'

Bess sank into a deep curtsey. 'Lady Marchant.'

Louise waved her fingers at Bess. 'No need for such formality, my dear. Here among my friends and family, I am simply Louise.' She cast a glance at Robin, one elegant eyebrow arched meaningfully. 'I trust the lovely Robin has been looking after you well?'

Bess giggled, her hand flying to her throat. Robin's face darkened.

The full force of Louise's attention now turned to Perdita. Perdita took a breath. This woman was truly beautiful, with thick gold hair and almond- shaped green eyes. Denzil stood looking at her with glazed eyes. Like a moth drawn to a candle, Perdita stared, unable to take her eyes from this woman. Little wonder that men were attracted to her

'Our kinswoman, Mistress Gray,' Joan said, the scowl firmly fixed between her brows. Clearly of all the company, Joan remained unmoved by Louise.

Louise allowed Perdita a cursory nod before looking around the room. 'I am frozen to the bone, Joan. I require a fire and sustenance.'

Joan gestured in the direction of the small, downstairs parlour. 'Both await you through here, Louise.'

A hastily lit fire struggled in the fireplace of the parlour and a dank, unseasonable chill still hung on the air. Louise's lip curled in barely concealed distaste.

'Denzil. A chair.' She waved a fine-boned hand in Denzil's direction and he scuttled forward pulling a chair toward the hearth. Louise sat, extravagantly arranging her damp scarlet skirts to best advantage. Everyone else remained standing,

She sighed extravagantly. 'This English weather. It almost makes me long for France.'

Perdita smiled as Joan ignored the whining. 'The queen was successful in her mission?' Joan enquired.

Louise turned to her and smiled. 'Very,' she said. 'With the arms she has brought with us, this affray should be over in no time.'

Ludovic entered bearing a tray of the same hearty fare that had satisfied a prince. Louise's nose twitched at the sight of the pastries and small ale.

'Had we had some notice of your arrival, Lady Marchant, we

would have prepared some more exciting delicacies,' Bess conciliated.

Louise flashed a smile in Bess's direction. 'We did not wish to waste time. Denzil, I will take that pastry.'

Denzil scurried forward, arranging a pastry on a platter and handing it to his wife. Whatever spell Louise had used to bind her husband to her will, it was a powerful one. Perdita had never believed in witches, but then she had never met Louise Marchant.

As Louise delicately picked at the pasty, she chattered about the wonders of France and the hardship of the journey back to England. Perdita wandered across to the window and stood looking out at the rain-swept landscape as Louise held court to her silent audience.

'Imagine, we were fired upon when we landed in Yorkshire. The queen, her very Majesty, had to cower in a ditch. Who are these upstart rebels that they should treat their king and queen in such a fashion?'

The rustle of petticoats drew her attention back to the room as Louise rose to her feet, brushing crumbs from her skirt.

'On the subject of upstart rebels. Where is Adam Coulter?'

Perdita answered for Joan. 'He is in his bed.'

Anger flashed across Louise's face. 'What do you mean?' She cast a glance at her husband. 'From what Denzil tells me, it has been nearly three weeks since he was wounded. He cannot still be abed?'

'His wound suppurated and he has suffered a serious relapse of wound fever,' Perdita lied.

She had no fear of Joan betraying the untruth, and out of the corner of her eye she saw Bess cast a curious glance at Robin. Robin answered with a shrug. Perdita breathed. They would confirm her tale.

'Robin is this true?' Louise rounded on Robin.

'We feared for his life on more than one occasion,' Robin responded without a flicker of an eye.

Louise narrowed her eyes. 'I am sorry to hear that. Robin, take me to his bedchamber.'

Robin glanced at Perdita and Perdita stepped forward. 'I will take you, Lady Marchant.'

With her heart in her mouth, Perdita opened the door to Adam's bedchamber and repressed a quick smile. The man who, half an hour previously, had been contemplating a ride to Warwick, now did a very convincing impression of a man on his death bed. He made a feeble effort to pull himself up on the bolsters as Louise swept in to the room.

'Louise, I thought I heard your voice,' he said in a weak voice. 'Looking magnificent as always. In fact, you've hardly changed.'

Louise stood at the end of the bed regarding him for a long moment, before she said, 'You on the other hand. I would not have recognised you. You have become quite the... what are they calling them, Denzil? Quite a roundhead.'

Adam's lips twitched as he looked past her. 'Denzil too. What a pleasing family reunion this is.'

Denzil glowered. 'What's this about a relapse? Robin's last report indicated you were well on the way to being fit enough to come to Oxford.'

Perdita glared at Robin who grimaced.

'Relapses are not uncommon, particularly when Captain Coulter was used so ill. I warned Colonel Marchant there was a risk of lung fever.'

Louise responded with a hiss and a wave of her hand.

Adam ignored her, his gaze seeking out Denzil. 'Even if I were fit to ride, I'm not going anywhere with you, Denzil. I take it you've not seen Prince Rupert?'

Denzil frowned. 'Rupert? No, we cut across Stratford to reach here. Why should that concern you?'

Adam reached under the bolster and held out the pass Rupert had signed.

'What's this?' Denzil took the paper and scanned it, the colour rising in his face.

'What nonsense is this?' Louise snatched the paper from him.

'It's what it says, Denzil,' Adam replied, a little strength coming back into his tone. 'The prince has revoked my parole and given me free pass to return to Warwick.'

'Robin?' Denzil rounded on his brother.

Robin held up a hand. 'It was not my doing,' he replied, and added in a low sulky tone. 'I was not to know that Adam and the prince were old comrades.'

'Denzil?' Louise's voice had a petulant edge. 'What does this mean?'

'It means, my dear, that Adam is a free man.'

Louise frowned. 'How?'

'He has evidently gulled Rupert into releasing him from his parole.'

'But how does he know Prince Rupert?' Louise frowned.

Robin retrieved the paper from her and returned it to Adam.

'The prince himself came here. It seems he and Adam served together in Germany,' Robin said. 'I could hardly prevent his visit.'

The colour in Denzil's face rose to an alarming puce.

'Is there nothing you can do?' Louise demanded of her husband.

Denzil shook his head. 'Nothing.'

Louise paced the room, her lips set in a hard line, her eyes narrowed. She stopped beside her husband and a smile curled her lip. A smile that made Perdita shiver and cross her forefinger and thumb, the sign against witches.

'But surely the parole does not apply if the charge is one of rape and murder?'

Denzil looked at his wife. 'What do you mean?'

Louise turned to face Adam. 'I mean, it is time Adam answered for his deeds that night. The old charges still stand.'

Perdita held her breath, not daring to look at Adam.

Even Denzil looked doubtful. 'That was so long ago, and—'

'And?' Louise's eyes blazed. 'I told you then and I repeat it now, I will see Adam Coulter hang yet for the murder of my brother.'

She cast Adam a look of such pure hatred that a shiver ran down Perdita's spine.

Adam met Louise's cold eyes with apparent equanimity. 'You would perjure yourself, to see me hang? You must hate me very much, Louise,' he said.

'You cannot even begin to imagine how much.' Louise closed her eyes and rubbed her temple. With a heavy sigh, she took her husband's arm. 'I had forgotten how tedious this man could be. Now, I have a headache. Joan, please show me to the best guest chamber. I think I may lie down for a little while.'

'Of course.' Joan looked solicitous. 'Your problems were always best solved on your bed, Louise.'

Louise darted Joan a malevolent glance before turning back on Adam. 'Lock the door on this man, Denzil. I do not trust him,' she snapped, and her gaze took in the Cliffords, 'or his friends.'

Now unquestionably a prisoner, Adam paced the bedchamber and swore under his breath. He had misjudged his timing. Far better to have let Denzil haul him off to Oxford and then produced the Prince's note. Now Rupert's intervention had proved pointless. His incarceration now had nothing to do with the war and a gentleman's honour and everything to do with Louise and the unfortunate death of her brother.

No one brought him any supper, and long after the house had

gone quiet he lay fully clothed on his bed, his hands behind his head, staring up at the bed hangings while he tried to think of how, in God's name, he was going to escape this particular knot.

Footsteps in the corridor outside his room brought him fully awake and he slipped off his bed. The key turned in the lock and the door creaked open. He held his breath, every nerve taut, as Denzil lurched into the room, carrying a single candle and a bottle. His brother pulled the door closed behind him and held up the candle. Seeing Adam, he put his finger to his lips.

'Denzil, this is an uncivilised hour to come calling,' Adam said.

Denzil set the candle and bottle on the table. 'You seem to have made a recovery since I last saw you,' he said, his words slurring slightly as Adam stepped out of the shadows and into the small illumination provided by the candle.

When Adam didn't answer, Denzil gestured at a chair beside the table. 'Sit down, Coulter, and drink with me.'

As Adam took the proffered chair, Denzil slumped into the chair opposite him and pushed the bottle across the table.

'Have some wine.'

There were no glasses so Adam pretended to take a swig. He needed his wits about him.

'Quite like old times, isn't it?' Denzil took the bottle from him, took a hefty draft and leaned back.

Adam regarded his brother with narrowed eyes. 'What is this about, Denzil?'

'Love.' Denzil heaved a sigh.

That had not been the answer Adam had been expecting. He sat back in his chair. 'Love?'

'Have you ever been in love?' Denzil began, and before Adam could answer, continued. 'Were you in love with Louise?'

Adam thought for a moment. No point in lying. 'At the time I thought I was,' he admitted.

'She's a witch.' Denzil swilled another mouthful of wine. 'She puts spells on men and they have to do her bidding. You were always into books and things. Wasn't there some witch who turned men into pigs?'

'Circe.'

'Yes,' agreed Denzil. 'Circe. Louise is like that. I know she is not a virtuous wife but I can't help it. I love her too much.' He took another swig and set the bottle down with cold deliberation. 'Have some more.'

'No, thank you,' Adam said.

'You didn't touch her, did you?'

'No,' Adam said. 'Strange how no one asked me that question at the time. You all assumed the first but nothing happened, and even if it had, it wouldn't have been rape. It doesn't excuse the fact that I intended to bed my brother's wife but trust me, Denzil, I didn't go to her bed without an invitation.'

Denzil grunted. 'And her brother?'

'Rolling drunk. He rushed at me with a drawn sword and fell on my weapon before I had a chance to step away.'

Denzil huffed out a heavy sigh. 'I've tried to hate you, but I can't. We share the same blood you and I. Even when you were a boy, you were always so much better at things than me.' He screwed up his face. 'You could have had any woman in court. Why Louise?'

Adam shrugged. What could he say? Nothing that would excuse the fact he intended to cuckold his brother.

'She crooked her finger and I followed. I'm not proud of that but I was young, Denzil.'

Denzil studied him from narrowed eyes. 'I s'pose I would have done the same thing if I'd been you. It's the sort of thing I would do. I'm not exactly a faithful husband. I've a boy you know?'

'Robin told me.'

'A little bastard like you. Louise won't let me bring him to Marchants so I pay his mother an allowance. He lives well enough.'

'What's his name?'

'Charles.' Denzil laid his head back against the chair. 'I'm a fool, Adam. A fool with a beautiful, venal woman for a wife who just has to click her fingers and I'm at her feet like a slathering lap dog.'

Adam leaned forward. 'Denzil, for what it's worth, if I had my time again...'

Denzil looked at him. 'Well, you had time to regret it, didn't you? I knew you weren't dead, you know. They wanted a ransom. I told Father not to pay it.' He frowned and pressed his right fore-finger to the surface of the table. 'No, that's not right. Louise persuaded me it was better to leave you to rot in Germany. I told everyone you were dead, even Father.'

Adam let a long silence pass between them and when he did speak, he kept his voice low and flat to hide the anger that welled inside him. 'You left me to rot? You let Father die thinking I was dead? I'm not sure whose crime is worse, Denzil.'

Denzil traced an imaginary line across the table top. 'I genuinely thought you were dead. I had a report that you had died of fever in Leipzig. Only found out you had survived after father had died and I had a letter telling me of your release.'

Liar, thought Adam as Denzil's gaze remained fixed on the table top.

'Do you have any idea what I endured in that accursed place?' Adam pushed back the sleeves of his shirt and held out his wrists to his brother. 'Do you know what these scars are? Manacles, Denzil. And there are other scars I could show you.' He broke off, the years of injustice and suppressed fury seething to the surface. 'You speak of being jealous of me, but do you have any idea what I had to do to make myself worthy of father's attention? Then you let him die thinking I was dead.'

He struggled to control his anger. Was that what Denzil was trying to do? Provoke him into violence?

He wouldn't—couldn't—give his brother and his wife that satisfaction.

He drew a long, slow steadying breath. 'As I see it, Denzil, the table between us is now clear of debt. I owe you nothing, nothing at all.'

Denzil toyed with the now empty wine bottle. 'You're right. I'm not proud of my actions, or my inactions,' he said, 'but I had Louise to consider. I do love her, you know.'

'So you say, but you're not in love with Louise,' Adam said. 'Not really. You're in lust with Louise. There is a huge difference. She has your balls in her vice and you just go where she leads you.'

'You're right of course. I would do anything for her. Anything,' Denzil said.

Adam fixed his stepbrother with an unblinking gaze. 'Even kill me?'

Denzil looked up at him from underneath his shaggy fringe and nodded, his face grim. 'Louise hates you.'

'I do know that,' Adam said with an ironic twist of his lips.

Denzil flung himself out of the chair and paced the room. He stopped, resting his knuckles on the table, and leaned forward, his face only inches from Adam's. 'Damn it. I should have just shot you when I had the chance. Saved us all this trouble.' He turned away and slumped back into his chair. 'You know what? I couldn't. I couldn't damn well shoot you in cold blood. You're my brother.' His shoulders slumped. 'In fact, I'm going to let you go.'

Adam raised an eyebrow.

Denzil waved a finger. 'Well, not me.' He tapped his forehead. 'I've had an idea. Get yourself ready to leave, Coulter. I'll be back shortly.'

Perdita slept badly, haunted by dreams of Louise's green eyes and a hangman's noose. In the dark of the night she awoke in a sweat to hear footsteps outside her door. The catch on her door jiggled. She lay motionless, rigid with terror as the door opened. Even in the dim light of the night candle that he carried, she recognised Denzil's bulky figure in the doorway and her heart raced with terror. Had he come to kill her, or worse?

The floorboards creaked as he walked across to the bed. He raised the candle and looked down at her. Perdita screwed her eyes tight, bracing herself for what was to come.

He shook her shoulder. 'I know you're awake. I want you to come with me,' he slurred.

She sat up, catching the bedclothes up to her chin, her voice unnaturally high and tight. 'What do you intend to do with me?'

He snorted. 'Don't fear, little Puritan, your virtue is quite safe with me, and neither do I intend to kill you, Mistress Gray, although God knows someone else may well want that privilege when we are done. Put some clothes on and come with me, now.'

Shivering from cold and apprehension, Perdita slipped from the bed, pausing only to pull on a petticoat and shoes. She threw a cloak around her shoulders for warmth and followed Denzil out into the corridor.

He put his fingers to his lips. 'Shhh. We mustn't wake her.'

Perdita had no intention of waking *her* but she shivered at the thought of Louise, hopefully slumbering peacefully in the best guest chamber at the farthest end of the corridor. They stopped outside the door to Adam's chamber. Denzil produced a key and gave it to Perdita.

'You. I've had far too much to drink.'

She opened the door and slipped inside the room. To her surprise, Adam sat in a chair at the table, fully dressed in cloak and hat. He started when he saw her and rose to his feet.

'What's she doing here?'

Perdita glanced at Denzil. 'What do you want of me?'

Denzil smiled, his fingers closing around Perdita's arm, drawing her in toward him.

'She's going to let you go. Someone must face Louise in the morning and I don't want it to be me or Robin or that pretty piece he's so keen on. It will be easy.' He bent his head to Perdita's ear. 'All you have to say, little Puritan, is that you had a spare key and you let him out.'

'I know I should be grateful to you, Denzil,' Adam said drily, 'But, as we have discussed, Louise is unforgiving and you're setting Perdita against her.'

Denzil looked at Perdita. 'You can go back to your bed, Puritan. I'll not have it said I forced you to something against your will.'

Perdita glanced from one brother to the other. How could two men who bore the same blood be so different? Were they two sides of the same coin, the opposite and yet the same?

'I'm not scared of Louise,' she lied. 'I'll take the blame, my lord.'

Denzil threw his arm across Perdita's shoulders. 'See, she'll do it, and what does it matter if she earns Louise's undying hatred? She'll be in good company. Those people she can't use, she hates. Louise's philosophy of life is quite simple.'

Adam looked across at her, his eyes dark shadows in the inadequate light. She wanted to tell him that she would walk through the very fires of hell if it meant she could see him free.

'Good,' Denzil said. 'Well, are you going?'

Adam stood up. 'What about your men?'

'Sleeping like babies in the barn. There's no one in the stables. Take Rob's horse. It's the fastest.'

Adam smiled. 'Rob will never forgive me.'

Denzil shrugged. 'I saw Rob's eyes tonight. He'd rather see you free than dancing at the end of the hangman's noose.' He stretched, 'God's death but I'm tired. I'm going to bed. I'll see you in the morning, Mistress Gray.'

'I have no doubt you will be suitably outraged,' Perdita said.

Adam put a hand on his brother's arm. 'Lay a finger on her and you answer to me.'

Denzil straightened with drunken dignity. 'You have my word as a gentleman.' He bowed and lurched out of the room.

Perdita glanced at the sky beyond the window, already showing a faint lightening of dawn. 'There's not much time, Adam.'

He nodded and caught her arm, drawing her toward him. 'Perdita, how many times can one person be indebted to another?'

'What do you mean?'

'By my calculation, this is the third time you have saved my life. What can I do to repay you?'

Her eyes met his. 'Nothing, Adam. Perhaps one day the debt can be repaid but not here and now.' She wriggled out of his grasp. 'You must go. Does your leg need redressing before you leave?'

He shook his head. 'It'll do.'

As they turned for the door, she took his hand and turned it over so it was palm up. 'This is for you.'

He turned over the ancient locket, her mother's only piece of jewellery.

He flicked open the catch, revealing the lock of dark brown hair curled within it.

'Take it,' she said, looking up at him.

Her body ached for him to take her in his arms, and as if reading the longing in her gaze, he drew her toward him, his arm circling her waist, pressing her to him, forcing her to look up at him.

Perdita closed her eyes and surrendered to his lips, her passion matching his with a bruising intensity. His fingers meshed in her hair and her whole body tingled and ached for him. Even as she surrendered to the powerful need to be his arms, a wave of guilt swept through her. Why did she not feel like this when Simon kissed her?

As if he sensed her thoughts, he released her and in a swift movement he fastened the locket around his neck, turned on his heel, and with his boots in his hand, Adam was gone.

The barest shimmer of light lifted the dark beyond the windows. Perdita shivered and drew her cloak around her. She tiptoed back to her room, flung herself down on the bed, and prepared for the storm that would surely engulf the house when Louise discovered her prey had escaped her.

Perdita did not consider herself a coward, but even as she descended the stairs to the sound of Louise's voice raised in anger coming from the parlour her courage failed her and she considered returning to the safety of her own chamber with the door locked.

But she had promised Denzil, and in the dark of the night, Denzil had showed himself to be, at heart, a decent human being. Louise had to be faced.

Taking a deep breath Perdita walked in on an ugly scene. Louise's hair was in disarray, and her face contorted with rage. Denzil by contrast looked pale but composed.

'Louise, for the love of the good Christ, I have a headache,' he said.

'Is there something amiss?' Perdita enquired, schooling her face to the well-practiced neutrality she had employed in dealing with her husband.

'He's gone,' Louise shrieked.

'I know.' Perdita laid the key Denzil had given her on the table in front of Louise.

Louise's eyes blazed. 'How dare you interfere?'

She raised her hand but Denzil caught it as Perdita took a step back, anticipating the blow.

Louise shot her husband a look of pure fury but her hand fell. Straightening, she pushed her hair back behind her ears and took a deep breath as if bringing her surging emotions back under control. She swallowed, and with narrowed eyes advanced on Perdita. 'What gave you the right to interfere in this matter? It is no business of yours.'

Perdita struggled to keep her features neutral, although her heart pounded and her guts surged like water. Samuel Gray was a lamb compared to this wolf in woman's clothing.

Carefully avoiding Denzil's eyes, Perdita fixed on the beautiful face and glittering eyes of Louise. 'God willed me to do it. He spoke to me in the night and told me that what you were planning was against his will.'

Louise stared at her. 'God? What has God to do with this?'

Perdita placed a pious hand on her breast. 'God wished to remind you of his holy writ. "Thou shalt not bear false witness", and I truly believe that is what you planned in your heart, Lady Marchant.'

Louise paled and her breath escaped between half-opened lips. Her hand reached for the back of a chair. Her gaze locked with Perdita, the hatred in her eyes burning through to Perdita's soul.

'I'll not forget this, Mistress Gray.'

A cold chill ran down Perdita's spine and once more she found herself making the sign against witches.

Louise straightened, patting her disordered curls back into some semblance of order. She shot a glance at her husband. 'Denzil, Her Majesty is expecting me this morning. I'm leaving.' Without a backward glance at Perdita she left the room.

Before Perdita could speak, Robin burst through the door, his face flushed, his hat in his hand. 'Sorry, Denzil, no sign of him. He must have been gone hours. He took my horse too. We'll never catch him before he makes Warwick.'

Denzil made a show of banging his fist on the table. 'God rot him. Nothing for it Rob, the queen is moving on today so we must be gone. Go and ready the men.'

Robin saluted and turned on his heel, no longer Bess's lovesick swain but a soldier.

Alone together, Perdita and Denzil stared at each other.

'You played your part well,' Denzil said at last.

Perdita reached for the table to steady herself. She took a deep breath. 'You're a coward, Denzil Marchant.'

'Absolutely,' he agreed, bowed and was gone.

Perdita sank into a chair. The events of the last few weeks had turned her world upside down and a hundred conflicting emotions surged in her mind. A tear escaped, dribbling down her cheek, and as the strain of the interview with Louise took hold, she laid her head on her arms and allowed the tears to fall.

She started at a light touch on her shoulder, jumping to her feet to face Joan.

'Excuse me,' she managed to say as she dashed at her swollen eyes.

'Are you going to tell me what really happened?' Joan asked. 'Just as well Adam can't see you now.'

Perdita sniffed and dashed at her swollen eyes. 'Why?'

'Some women like Louise can cry and still look perfect. You're not one of them.'

Perdita managed a smile. 'He should be safely in Warwick by now.'

Joan picked up the key Perdita had laid on the table. 'How did you come by this? I thought Denzil had it.'

'It was Denzil who freed him. I just took the blame.'

'Denzil?' Joan's eyes widened. 'It would seem I have misjudged my nephew. He does still have some of his own will left.'

'Up to a point.' Perdita snorted and then closed her eyes. 'You should have seen her, Joan. If she could have struck me dead on the spot she would have done so.'

Joan drew in an audible breath and nodded. 'You have made a formidable enemy in Louise, I'm afraid.'

'Adam is gone, and I,' she faltered. 'I am to wed Simon so there should be no further need of her enmity.'

'Ah yes, Simon,' Joan said. 'He seems to have become somewhat lost in the events of the last few days. Tell me, Perdita, do you love him?'

Perdita hesitated a fraction too long. 'Of course I do. How can you ask? Now excuse me. It was a long night and I feel the need to rest.'

'Of course you do,' Joan echoed Perdita's assertion as Perdita walked from the room.

As if he had been summoned, Simon returned a few days later, claiming a few day's reprieve from his duties with Lord Northampton.

Perdita regarded her betrothed with critical eyes. His drawn and troubled face worried her. It was not just the physical changes that troubled her. Each time she saw him all his confident optimism seemed to have further leeched from him.

'Simon you're becoming quite thin,' she remarked, attempting to keep her tone light.

'The food can be a little scarce at times.' He shrugged and looked around his own pleasant parlour. 'I heard you had an unwelcome guest.'

'Unwelcome?'

'That man, Coulter.'

'He's Joan's nephew and he'll never be unwelcome in her house, whatever the circumstances.'

Simon flushed and drew a weary hand over his eyes. 'I'm sorry, Perdita. It is a strange world we are living in. Bess tells me he escaped his brother's clutches? Some story about Prince Rupert?'

Perdita nodded. 'Indeed. The prince came in person. It would seem they had served together in Germany.'

'Rupert? Here? At the behest of Adam Coulter?' Simon's tired eyes came to life.

Perdita smiled and nodded. 'Would I lie?'

'Well, I'll be damned. As I said, strange times indeed.'

'I might add that the prince is every bit as impressive as his legend.'

Simon nodded. 'He has the women swooning at his feet.' He leaned forward and took her hands in his. 'Perdita, this damnable war is set to continue for some time yet.'

'So it would seem, Simon.'

He looked wretched. 'I have no way of knowing when I can be with you. Are you sure you want to go through with this wedding?'

'Of course I do,' she said fiercely and forced herself to laugh. 'Anyway, it is too late, Simon. The tailor has been sent for and the dress is ordered.'

He smiled at last. 'The dress, eh? Tell me about it?'

'Midnight blue damask. It will be quite the most beautiful dress I have ever owned and I will not see it lie in a chest, waiting for you to make up your mind exactly when we are to be wed.'

'Colonel Compton seems happy to grant me a few days leave at Christmas time. It will be very quiet, Perdita. Although I have invited Will Compton. I hope you don't mind.'

'Of course not. I'm not one for large pageants, Simon.'

He frowned. 'Now tell me about this Robin Marchant? From the way Bess talks of him, do I detect that they have developed something of a liaison?'

'Thrown together for weeks as they were, what do you expect?'

'Perdita. I trust you saw that nothing improper occurred.'

Perdita smiled. 'I could not be with them all the time.'

Simon huffed. 'I always said Bess had the right to choose. I would never force her to marry against her will. Now am I supposed to approve or disapprove?'

'What a question. Robin is a delightful young man who could have the choice of any court beauty he wishes, but he has chosen Bess.'

'It is just that everything to do with the Marchants seems so difficult.'

'I think Robin is the exception.'

'Then perhaps it would be sensible if I were to have an opportunity to talk with him. When next I'm in Oxford I'll seek him out.' Simon rose wearily to his feet. 'I must get to my bed. I'm expected back in Banbury tomorrow.' He pulled her to her feet, and stood facing her, holding her hands in his. 'Only a few months, Perdita, and we will be man and wife. It seems like a dream.'

He leaned forward and kissed her, a hesitant, chaste kiss. Perdita waited for the answering tide of passion that had swept over her when Adam had taken her in his arms but it did not come. She laid her head against Simon's shoulder and the guilt trickled from her in her tears. She knew Simon would mistake them for sadness at his departure. Let him think that. She would marry him and forget what might have been with Adam Coulter.

Chapter Ten

PRESWOOD HALL, 15 DECEMBER 1643

Winter came and the campaigning slowed, lost in mud, rain and snow, but at Preswood, a sense of anticipation had begun to build as the day of Perdita and Simon's wedding approached. They had decided on the 20th of December with the hope that Simon would be able to stay long enough to enjoy Christmas.

With the cold, the women had abandoned the great parlour for the smaller, more easily warmed downstairs parlour where they passed the days when not busy with household chores. Joan kept to her own chamber and Bess confided that Joan was working on a painting, a wedding present, and was anxious to have it finished before the day.

Bess and Perdita were engaged on stitching a fine piece of linen Bess had found in an old chest to make a table cloth. The peremptory fall of the great brass door knocker made them both jump and even before Ludovic appeared at the door of the parlour with a mud-spattered courier, wearing the regimental blue of Simon's regiment, Perdita knew he brought only bad news.

The soldier bowed and held out a letter.

'I have a message for thee, Mistress Gray, from Colonel Compton.'

Perdita took the letter, her heart pounding beneath her bodice. She thanked him and told Ludovic to see that the soldier received refreshment in the kitchen.

Alone with Bess she stared at the letter in her hand, the blood red wax imprinted with Compton's seal unbroken. A year of war had taught them that a personal letter from Simon's commander at Banbury could only bring ill news.

'Perhaps it is to say that he is coming to the wedding?' Even Bess's voice wavered.

Perdita looked up at her and shook her head. 'No, Bess. It won't be that.'

Bess's hands going to her mouth as she stifled a sob. 'Open it, Perdita,' she instructed.

Barely able to control her trembling, Perdita broke the seal, the hastily penned words dancing illegibly across the page.

'Read it! For the love of God, read it!' Bess blurted out.

Perdita forced herself to focus, reading the missive aloud.

'My dear Mistress Gray, I fear that this missive brings you bad news but not the very worst you could expect. Simon Clifford is, to the best of my intelligence, alive and well when last seen. Sadly for your happy plans, an event to which we were all looking forward, a week has passed since Captain Clifford was taken by the forces of parliament and is, I believe, immured in Warwick Castle. No doubt the foul fiends will be looking for some sort of ransom to deliver him safely to your hands as they have in the past. I have written personally to the Governor of Warwick Castle putting your case and I pray yet that we can secure his release forthwith in time for your wedding. Yr Faithful Servant W. Compton.'

Perdita set the letter down on the table and looked at Bess. 'What are we going to do?'

'Adam Coulter is at Warwick.' Bess enunciated the name, her

eyes bright with hope. 'Perdita he owes you his life. Go to him and secure Simon's release.'

A thousand turbulent emotions poured into Perdita's heart. In the months since he had ridden away from Preswood, there had been no word from Adam. While she told herself that she had no wish to see him, the memory of that stolen embrace, that shared moment of intimacy still haunted her dreams.

She had no choice. He was the only hope that she had.

She took the letter and went in search of Joan, making sure she announced her presence in time for Joan to secure her secret project.

Joan read the letter, her mouth tightening.

'At least we can thank God Simon is still alive,' Joan said. 'Bess is right, Perdita. You must go to Warwick and speak with Adam. His debt is to you, not to Bess nor I.'

Joan rose stiffly from her chair and unlocked a heavy wooden chest that stood beneath the window. She withdrew two small leather pouches, weighed them thoughtfully in her hand and without looking at Perdita said, 'What price a man's life, Perdita?'

'Joan. I have some coin. I don't need yours.'

Joan shook her head and pressed the bags into Perdita's hand. 'This is Simon's inheritance. I have no need of it. Take it. Simon's life and happiness is worth more to me than gold.'

Adam sighed and drew another piece of paper towards him. Another claim for compensation from an aggrieved landowner that differed only from the previous ten he had read in the details.

'The 12th day of May Ano Dni 1643 one Creed Hopkins and Boovey attended with a troop of horse and men under the command of Captain

Joseph Hawkesworth came to the house of ye said Edward and then and there took out of ye stable there these horses following...'

Then followed a long list of items and amounts. Adam leaned back in his chair considering what to do with the claim. He could spare no money to settle this or any of them. He had no money to pay his own soldiers.

He did not even look up at a firm knock on the door.

'Come in,' he said abstractedly.

The door opened and Adam lowered the paper to see who had entered.

'Mistress Gray...Perdita!' he said, scrambling to his feet.

'Captain Coulter.' She responded only with a small bob and no smile of greeting. Her lips were blue and her hair hung in damp rats' tails from beneath the hood of her cloak, soaked from the sleeting rain outside.

When Perdita hesitated, casting a longing glance at the cosy fire that burned in the hearth, Adam rose and took her elbow, propelling her to the warmth.

Her teeth chattered and her gloved fingers fumbled ineffectually with the sodden knot that secured her cloak. He pushed her hands away and undid the cloak, laying it over a chair to dry. He placed a hand on her shoulder, easing her into a well-cushioned chair. She sat bolt upright staring into the fire with unseeing eyes.

'Perdita, you are half-frozen. Have you ridden from Preswood?'

She nodded and he hunkered down in front of her and pulled off her gloves, laying them on the hearth. He took her icy fingers between his hands and gently chaffed them. She winced and pulled her hands away, shaking them to restore the circulation.

'Now your boots.'

'I can...' she began, but he had already begun to pull off the mired riding boot. He looked up at her, holding one small, cold, damp foot cupped in his hand.

'Your stockings are saturated. Your feet will never warm. Take them off and set them before the fire.'

A faint colour stained her cheeks but she bent and removed her stockings, affording him a tantalising glimpse of ankle and well-turned calf before she drew her bare feet up underneath her. He fetched a blanket from his bed and swaddled her in it before bellowing to a servant to fetch some warm soup.

'What in God's name brings you here in this weather?' he chided.

'I had to see you on an important matter. I received—' She broke off as Adam's servant entered bearing a tray with soup, bread and wine which he set down on the table.

Adam dismissed him cursorily and turned back to Perdita, pleased to see a little colour returning to her face.

'Get this inside you.'

He handed her the bowl and spoon and she supped the soup, taking a couple of grateful gulps from the cup of wine he poured for her. Satisfied he had done all he could to make her comfortable, Adam flung himself into the chair opposite her. Resting his elbow on the arm of the chair, he leaned his face on his hand and regarded her thoughtfully.

'Better?'

She managed a faint smile. 'Much, thank you.'

'I trust you've not come alone?'

She shook her head. 'I left Ludovic at the inn and came straight here. They kept me waiting at the gate for simply ages before they let me in and I think that was only because they thought I was visiting you for entertainment.' A small smile touched the corners of her lips.

Adam smiled in response. 'There goes my reputation and yours.' His brow furrowed. 'So, what brings you here that is of such importance? It's not bad news? Joan?'

Perdita shook her head. 'No, everyone is well enough. And you, Adam? You have recovered?'

He shrugged. 'My leg troubles me in this weather and those damned ribs ache in the cold but otherwise I'm fine.'

'You sound like an old man.'

'In truth there are times when I feel like one, Perdita .' He ran a hand through his hair. 'There are too many young men about who make me feel like the old and grizzled veteran that I am.'

That small smile appeared again and a glint shone in her eye. 'Rest assured, you do not look old and grizzled.'

'Thank you for saying that, but I can see for myself that there are grey hairs at my temple. So if it is not bad news and you are not here merely to enquire after my health, I will ask you again, what has brought you to Warwick in this foul weather, Perdita?'

Any trace of humour slipped from her face. Her grave, brown eyes rested on his face. 'You have Simon.'

'Simon? What do you mean, I have Simon?'

Her eyes widened and the brown eyes flashed. 'You're no fool, Adam, as deputy governor of this castle, you must know who you have immured in your dungeons.'

He shook his head. 'I've been in London these last few weeks and did not return until yesterday.'

Perdita stood up and took two leather pouches from her skirts. They clinked as she laid them on the table on top of the sheaf of papers he had been considering.

'There is your ransom. Please restore Simon to me.'

He rose to his feet and stood quite still, staring down at the two bags of coin. What sort of man did she think he was? In an angry gesture he swept the coins to the floor where they landed with a thunk.

He looked up at her, hurt and indignation seething in his chest. 'God's death, Perdita, who do you take me for?'

Her gaze met his, her brown eyes wide with anger and her

colour high. 'One of the foul fiends of Warwick Castle who hold men's lives for ransom I think is how Colonel Compton put it.'

She may as well have slapped his face. He took a step back.

After all they had been through together, she should think him no more than a 'foul fiend'?

He bent and picked up the moneybags, handing them back to her. 'I'll not take your money for Simon Clifford's life.'

Her fingers closed on the coins and she quivered. 'Are you refusing to release him to me, Adam?'

He shook his head. 'I told you once I owed you for my life, Perdita Gray. I will gladly restore Simon to you, without the need for recompense.' He glanced at the window. 'It's getting late and I need to find him. Come back in the morning. If he is indeed here I will give him to you then.'

Perdita looked away. Her shoulders rose and fell in a silent sigh. 'Thank you. We are to be wed in four days.'

A cold hand clenched Adam's heart. 'About time.' He forced the words out between stiff lips.

He looked away as Perdita pulled on her damp stockings and boots. Pausing only to collect her cloak and gloves, she left his room without a backward glance.

Adam sank back into his chair, staring at the door as it slammed shut behind her. He remembered the feel of her in his arms, the touch of her lips on his, and reminded himself that once again he had done the unthinkable, fallen in love with a woman who belonged to another man. This time he would make no mistake.

Adam stared at the door that led down to the dungeons of Warwick Castle. They were old, probably older than the present structure that stood over them. Nothing had yet induced him to set foot beyond that door. The very thought of descending the narrow winding stairs below the castle made the sweat break out on the back of his neck and the breath tighten in his chest. It took very little to transport him back to Leipzig and the smell of unwashed bodies, and worse to bring back memories he saw only in his nightmares.

He hailed his sergeant who was supervising the mending and polishing of horse harness.

'Sir?'

'There is a prisoner below by the name of Simon Clifford. Bring him up for me.'

The sergeant saluted and without a moment's hesitation disappeared into the bowels of the castle, leaving Adam standing on the damp, cold cobbles, hoping that his men did not notice how his hands shook.

He kicked at a loose stone, unable to shed the pall that thoughts of his own incarceration resurrected. He had little memory of how he had made his way from Leipzig to Paris, except that every day had been a desperate fight for survival. He had begged and he had stolen, and had occasionally earned a few honest pennies with his drawing, but there had been times he had despaired of ever seeing England again.

Mercifully in Paris he had found Marie, the plump, cheerful whore who had warmed his bed in the early days of his exile. She had since married, her friends at the bawdy house had told him. Married or not, she had taken him in, nursed him back to health and provided him with clothes and the money for a fare back to England. He had repaid the money but he would be forever in her debt as he was in Perdita's.

I must have looked like that when they brought me back into the light, Adam thought as Simon Clifford stumbled out of the doorway assisted by a none-too-gentle shove from the sergeant. Simon gathered himself up and stood for a moment, blinking as his eyes adjusted to the grey, wintry light. He has only been down there for a matter of days, thought Adam.

Imagine three years, Simon Clifford.

Simon's gaze came to rest on Adam.

'Coulter. I can't tell you how good it is to see a familiar face. I asked for you, but they told me you were away from the castle.'

Adam bowed. 'My apologies, Clifford. I've just returned from London. If I'd known of your incarceration I would have at least seen you somewhat more comfortably housed.' He gestured at the gate. 'As it is you are free to go.'

'Free?' Simon's mouth fell open and his eyes widened.

'I believe you have a wedding to attend. You will find your bride waiting for you by the postillion gate.'

Simon took two steps and stumbled. Adam caught his arm and stayed his fall.

'Steady.'

'Sorry, just a bit dizzy,' Simon mumbled, rubbing his eyes.

A cold dread washed over Adam. He had received reports that in his absence the inevitable sickness had broken out among the prisoners and that a couple had died. The man's colour seemed unnaturally high and his eyes bright with fever. What if Simon had contracted the prison fever?

He slipped his arm under Simon's shoulders.

'It's all right.' Simon's words slurred. 'It's just a headache. I can walk.'

'You have a wedding in a few days,' Adam said, steering Simon in the direction of the gate. 'Perdita will make quite sure you are well by then.'

'Oh yes, the wedding.' Simon hefted a sigh and looked up at Adam, his eyes bright with more than just fever. 'I love her so much, Coulter.'

'I'm sure she knows that,' Adam forced the words out.

'She's so beautiful. Don't you think?'

'Yes,' agreed Adam. 'She is the most beautiful woman I have ever met.'

'I'm a lucky man.'

You don't know how lucky, Adam agreed.

After the rain of the previous day, a heavy winter fog enveloped the castle, giving it the impression of a mythological Camelot, rising out of the marsh. Perdita and Ludovic had been waiting nearly an hour, stamping their feet and moving as much as they could to stop from freezing to the spot.

'I see them, mistress,' Ludovic said at last.

Out of the fog, two figures emerged from the postilion gate, one tall and straight, his dark head bare, his arm around a shorter stooped figure. Perdita picked up her skirts and ran up the causeway, calling Simon's name.

Adam released his grip on the prisoner and Simon stumbled toward her. She took him in her arms, filthy and reeking as he was.

'Perdita,' he mumbled. 'How good you smell.'

'I wish I could say the same of you,' she chided.

Over Simon's head, she caught Adam Coulter's cold, hard gaze.

Hypocrite, his eyes seemed to say. How can you profess to love this man when it is me you want?

Abruptly he turned on his heel, swallowed up by the shadows of the gatehouse. Perdita turned her attention back to her betrothed. He looked appallingly ill, nearly two week's growth of beard could not hide the hollowed cheeks and sunken eyes, and a quick touch of his forehead confirmed her worst fear. He had a fever.

'Simon, are you well enough to ride?

He smiled at her, his finger tracing the line of her cheekbone. 'I'm all the better for seeing you, Perdita. It's just a chill.' He cast a quick glance up at the forbidding walls of Warwick Castle. 'Come let us get away from this place. I have a wedding to attend, I believe.'

They were greeted at Preswood by Bess, who must have been watching for them. She ran to her brother's side as Simon slid off his horse and leaned against the animal's flank.

'It's good to be home,' he said with a smile for his sister.

'Simon. How wonderful. Perdita, you did it!'

Ludovic lifted Perdita down from her horse and she crossed to Simon.

'It is Adam Coulter we must thank,' she said. 'He released him without recourse to ransom.'

'I should think so too.' Bess put her arm around her brother, peering anxiously into his haggard face.

'Are you all right, Simon?'

Simon gathered himself and took a few steps. He staggered and she caught his arm.

'I'm fine,' he said. 'Just a little tired.'

Perdita touched his cheek and shook her head. 'Simon, you're burning up. I told you, you have a fever.'

His mouth drooped. 'I'm sorry, Perdita I didn't want to worry you. I do have a headache. It started yesterday and I do not seem able to shake it. In truth there were moments on the road when I doubted I would make it home.'

'Oh Simon, you can't be ill,' wailed Bess. 'The wedding. The banns have been called.'

'I shall be hale by the wedding,' her brother said with what he no doubt thought was a reassuring smile. It gave his face a twisted ghoulish look and despite herself, Perdita shivered. A premonition as cold as the fog that still enshrouded them touched her shoulder.

'A bath and my own bed and I will be a new man.' Simon took

Perdita's hand. 'Now I'm here with you. Good of Coulter to let me go like that. What did you say to him?'

'He has proved himself a good friend. Now let's get you cleaned up and into bed,' she said, slipping an arm around his waist.

The redoubtable Ludovic was already by her side. Under his firm guidance, Simon was bathed and put to bed with a warm brick and a dose of one of Perdita's febrifuges.

But by the next morning, Simon had a high fever, and he shook so violently his teeth chattered. More worryingly a rash had begun to spread across his body. Perdita sent for a doctor from Stratford who looked at Simon, bled him and confirmed Perdita's worst fear.

'You say he's been a prisoner at Warwick? I have had reports of fever among the prisoners there.' He paused. 'Spotted fever.'

Perdita took a deep breath. Her father had been an apothecary in London where spotted fever was not uncommon. It ravaged towns and armies where too many bodies were forced into close contact with each other. Unless God was merciful, the doctor may as well have delivered a death sentence.

Hardly knowing what to say, Perdita shared the news with Joan and Bess and gave orders they were both to stay away. She and Ludovic would see to Simon's nursing.

'But you, Perdita,' Bess said. 'You don't want to catch it.'

Perdita lifted a face devoid of hope. 'What does it matter, Bess?'

If she contracted the fever, no one would grieve.

By the evening, Simon's fever had worsened into delirium. Ludovic's grim face confirmed her diagnosis. He too had seen it too many times to have any doubts.

'Is there nothing we can do?' Perdita pleaded. 'Should we send for the doctor again?'

Ludovic shook his head. 'There is nothing he can do except pray.'

On the third day it was clear that unless the fever broke, it would kill Simon. Even Ludovic's extreme measures of fresh air and cold water proved no assistance. Simon's moments of lucidity came more rarely and he tossed and turned so violently that it took both Ludovic and Perdita to subdue him.

In the darkest hours of the night that should have been her wedding night, Perdita maintained her vigil by his bed. She slept, sitting in a chair, her face in her arms on the bed.

She awoke with a start at the touch of a hand on her hair.

'Simon?' she blinked up at him.

'You're so lovely,' he whispered.

Hope sprang into Perdita's heart. Had the fever broken at last? But when she held the light to his face, she saw the shadow of death in the face of the man who was to have been her husband.

'Perdita?'

'Dearest.'

'I'm dying. Don't lie. I can see it in your face.'

'It's the spotted fever,' she said quietly. 'Some do recover from it.'

'Some, but not many,' Simon whispered. 'Perdita, I would have seen you as my bride.'

'You will yet,' Perdita said fiercely.

'No,' he sighed. 'In the last year I have seen more death than any man should see in a lifetime and I know I'm dying. My only regret is that I must leave you.'

Tears filled her eyes. She clutched his hand, holding on to the life of this dear good man.

'I like to think we would have got on well together, even if you don't love me.'

'Simon, you can't say that.' Her voice shook. 'I do love you and I want nothing more than to be with you. The thought of life without you is more than I can bear.'

They were not empty words, meant to cheer a dying man. She knew as she spoke that they were the absolute truth. She may not have loved Simon as she loved Adam Coulter, but that did not make her feelings for Simon anything less than love.

His gaze held hers, seeking the veracity of her words. He knows me better than I thought, Perdita realised. He knows that my eyes would never lie.

'I'm sorry, Perdita,' he whispered. 'I wanted the world for you.' His fingers tightened on hers with a fierce urgency. 'I'll not leave you as you were left before. That is my last promise to you.'

'What do you mean by that?' Perdita leaned over him, but he had already slipped into unconsciousness and she could no longer reach him. She bent over and kissed him gently on his ravaged cheek.

'Simon. Believe me, I want nothing from you except that you live.'

The tears spilled from her eyes and fell onto Simon's hand.

With a heavy heart she woke Bess and Joan to come and sit with her.

Simon's death was, as his life had been, quiet and gentle. His soul slipped into the darkest hour just before dawn.

Bess wept copiously into Joan's arms, but Perdita had no more tears, only a dull and fearful emptiness filled her. After Bess had been put to bed with a sleeping draught, Perdita knelt by Simon's bed and prayed for the soul of the man who had loved her so dearly but whose love she could never return in full.

In the days following Simon's death, Joan and Bess wept, but not so Perdita. She had endured the funeral in dry-eyed silence. Now she stood at the window of the great parlour looking out but not seeing the cheerless, wintry landscape,

What am I, she thought, *a widow who was never a wife? An unnat-*

ural creature who cannot weep for the man who was to be your husband, a man who loved you without condition. A man who never knew you loved another.

'This is God's punishment,' she whispered, leaning her forehead against the cold, unforgiving glass.

'Did you say something, Perdita?'

Perdita turned to look at Joan. 'I should be the one who is dead, Joan.'

Joan rose to her feet, reaching for her stick. She hobbled across to Perdita. She stamped the edge of her cane on the wooden floor.

'Enough of this maudlin self-pity, Perdita.' Joan's lips compressed in a tight line. 'You are not the first woman to lose a loved-one to this accursed war. God is no more punishing you than you than any other woman. Until the men come to their senses, the killing will go on, the death will go on. We need you to be strong.'

The force of Joan's anger caused Perdita to take a step back. She was tired of being strong. She needed someone to take the burden of responsibility from her, not heap more responsibilities on to her shoulders. She closed her eyes, acknowledging the deep longing she had been supressing for months.

She needed—she wanted— Adam Coulter.

But she had no time to respond to Joan as Ludovic announced the arrival of the family lawyer from Stratford. Perdita drifted across to the fire and took a seat. As the lawyer droned in the background, his voice a monotone, she stared into the fire, drawn in to its cheerful crackling.

'Perdita. Perdita aren't you listening?' Bess's insistent voice broke into her reverie.

'Hmm?' She looked up at the lawyer.

The man cleared his throat and repeated.

'Master Clifford recently changed his will. He left a substantial dowry for his sister Elizabeth and of course the right of residence and an allowance to his stepmother, but he has left to Perdita Gray the entire estate of Preswood until death or marriage, after which the estate would revert to his sister, her heirs and successors.'

Perdita looked from the lawyer to Joan and Bess. 'But we were never wed. I have no rights.'

'The provisions were not conditional upon your wedding.' The lawyer coughed. 'Master Clifford was most insistent on that point.' He rose to his feet and reached for his hat. 'I will draw up all the necessary papers and bring them to you within the week. I bid you good day, ladies.'

After he had gone, accompanied by Joan, Bess and Perdita stared at each other.

'I don't know what to say,' Perdita faltered. 'I can't accept the terms of Simon's will. All of this should be yours by right, Bess.'

Bess wrinkled her nose. 'And what use would I make of it? Simon has left me amply endowed, and God willing I will be wed.' She knelt in front of Perdita and took her hands. 'This is a secret, but Robin has asked me to marry him and I have accepted. Robin has lands and estates in his own right.'

Tears caught in Perdita's throat. So long in coming, it seemed it now took the smallest provocation to produce a flood and she fell into her Bess's arms, weeping.

When the flood had subsided to hiccups, Bess disengaged her, looking at her with a furrowed brow. 'I didn't mean to upset you so.'

Perdita shook her head. 'Not crying for Simon,' she managed. 'Tears of happiness for you. You and Robin are entirely right for each other.'

Bess flushed. 'I think so too. We do not intend to make it public knowledge yet, particularly so soon after Simon's death.' She took Perdita's hand. 'Fate has dealt you some bitter blows, Perdita. Recognise a change in your fortunes and rejoice in them.'

Perdita dashed at her tears, taking the kerchief that Bess gave her. 'Your brother had the truest heart of any man I've ever known, Bess. I wish he was with me still. I wish that I could throw my arms around his neck and kiss him, tell him how much I truly loved him. All the money in the world will not bring him back or take this pain from my heart.'

Bess laid a hand on Perdita's shoulder. 'We both lost someone we loved, but time will heal the hurt.'

Perdita lowered her head. 'Time,' she echoed. 'Do we have time, Bess?'

Chapter Eleven

Adam shook the snow from his hat and cloak and tried, unsuccessfully, to remove the worst of the mud from his boots before he knocked on the door.

The man seated at the table raised a tired, drawn face. 'Who are you?'

'Coulter,' Adam said. 'I've brought the supplies from Warwick. We would have been here sooner but the wagons bogged in the roads.'

Sir Thomas Fairfax's face lifted. Black Tom, Adam had heard Fairfax called, and the dark saturnine looks and thin, scholar's face did not give lie to the nickname. In the tired eyes the fire of the man burned, that spark that differentiated him and would make every man who wore his colours follow him despite their ragged clothes and lack of rations. They were much of an age but Adam felt he was in the presence of a man of many more years, already worn down by the responsibilities thrust upon him.

Sir Thomas gestured at the fire. 'Come and stand by the fire. The weather outside is foul.'

Adam took a place in front of the cheerful blaze and closed his eyes as the warmth permeated his frozen, aching bones.

'Take this.' Fairfax poured him a cup of wine and joined him by the fire. 'You're most welcome, Captain Coulter. If you've seen any of my men, you will know how desperate our situation is.'

Adam set the cup down and fumbled in his jacket, pulling out a crumpled paper, the same crumpled paper, which Colonel Purefoy had, with some grumbling, consented to sign. He handed it to Fairfax.

'I have served in the low country and the Palatinate. I have here a recommendation from Colonel Purefoy, should you have need of a field officer of my experience.'

Fairfax took the paper and broke the seal. He studied the contents and looked up at Adam. 'Purefoy speaks highly of you, Coulter. Why would you wish to leave Warwick?'

'I am wasted in the garrison, sir. Since Lord Brooke's death last year, there is nothing to hold me at Warwick.'

Fairfax set Purefoy's letter down amongst the scattered papers on the table and nodded. 'I do indeed have need of an officer of such experience, Coulter...several officers in fact. I have a regiment of horse wanting a good major. Would you take that?'

'I would be honoured, sir,' Adam said and bowed.

He had not been telling an untruth when he had told Fairfax that garrison life galled, but in truth he had no heart to remain in Warwickshire. He had marked Perdita and Simon's wedding day by getting appallingly drunk, and in the weeks that followed had taken any task Purefoy gave him to get him out from behind the castle walls. He had jumped at the opportunity to take this convoy of much needed supplies to the beleaguered parliamentary forces in the north, and had persuaded Purefoy to release him should Fairfax have a use for him.

Fairfax looked around the room of the pleasant house he had taken as his headquarters. 'I had hoped to make Gainsborough our winter quarters, but I have this day,' he gestured at the paper on the table, 'received orders from my father to relieve Nantwich. The Irish have landed. They mean to reinforce Byron and undo our work in Lancashire and Yorkshire. We march in the morning. I am afraid that leaves you little time to become acquainted with your new command.'

He picked up his pen and scrawled on a blank piece of paper which he folded and sealed, handing it to Adam. 'Your orders, Coulter. You will find Captain Hewitson lodging at the sign of the Swan. My compliments to him. I present his new major.' Fairfax sat back in his chair. 'You have a northern name, Coulter, but you don't speak like a man of the north.'

Adam shook his head. 'My childhood home was in Leicestershire, sir.'

'I give you fair warning, you'll not have an easy time of it. The men of the north are loyal to their own and you're an outsider. You must prove yourself worthy of the men you lead.'

Adam nodded. 'I'm equal to whatever task you set me, sir.'

A smile lifted Fairfax's dark countenance. 'If what Purefoy tells me is the truth then I don't doubt it, Coulter.'

Fairfax had been right. Acceptance of an outsider had to be earned, and while Adam did not face outright hostility, he was left in no doubt that the regiment had expected the dour Yorkshireman, Obadiah Hewitson to have been given the command. They obeyed Adam without question but without enthusiasm as they trudged through the bitter weather towards Cheshire and Nantwich.

At Fairfax's headquarters, his staff bent over the map on the table.

'My intelligence tells me that Byron has split his forces on either side of the river.' Fairfax traced the line of the River Weaver. 'If the thaw comes, his force will be divided.'

'Do we intend to engage them?' Brereton asked.

Fairfax shook his head. 'We're facing a much greater force and the capability of the Irish veterans is unknown. My intention at this point is to strengthen the garrison at Nantwich and drive them back by attrition rather than show of strength. Richard?' He turned to his galloper, Richard Ashley. 'Where is that letter from that braggadocio, Lord Byron, we intercepted today?' Ashley handed him the paper. 'Gentlemen, this is who we are facing.'

Fairfax drew himself up to his full height, his lip curled in distaste as he read Byron's intercepted report out loud.

The assembled men listened in horror as Byron boasted of having slaughtered twenty civilians in the church at the village of Barthomley. After describing how his men had driven the villagers from refuge in the church tower by lighting a fire, he then recounted how twelve of them had been stripped. He had them all '...*put to the sword, which I find the best way to proceed with these kind of people* Byron concluded.

'What manner of man is this?' Brereton said in a hushed voice.

'The man we march to face tomorrow,' Fairfax said. 'Good night, gentlemen.'

Byron must have wondered what evil luck had beset him, as the next day the weather turned, melting the snow and thawing the frozen rivers, splitting his force. Intelligence reached the advancing parliamentarians that Byron knew of their advance and was making plans to meet them. Fairfax ordered his men into fighting order and, reinforced by the ragged veterans of Adwalton Moor, they continued the march toward Nantwich.

On a dark, wet, grey winter afternoon, in battle order, the parliamentary forces pushed forward through the hedgerows and narrow lanes. They were just north of the village of Acton when

Byron's infantry came on them in a flanking manoeuvre, attacking both the van and the rear guards. The bulk of Byron's force, including the cavalry would not be far behind but for the moment they were delayed by the terrain.

Fairfax wheeled his great white horse, his eyes bright. 'It seems our foe has found a way across the river. If he wants a battle, he shall have one. Coulter, take your men and aid with the rear-guard. We'll take our positions and deal with what lies before us.'

Adam returned to his men. He looked at their sullen faces but didn't have time for inspiring speeches. Now was the time for action. He glanced at Hewitson.

'To me,' he said. 'Let's take the scurvy, murdering devils.'

After the months of the tedium of garrison duties and convoy escorts, Adam's blood stirred and he heard once more the call to battle and knew the rightness of his cause.

He wheeled his horse and taking a hedge at the gallop, drew his sword. He heard the cry behind him and knew his men followed. Fairfax's rear-guard had been pushed back and were hard pressed as Adam's cavalry came up in their support. The foot soldiers made way, letting the horses through.

They hit the weary royalist infantry hard. Byron's men balked, wavered, and turned and ran. Adam stopped his men from going in pursuit, turning them back to go to the aid of the beleaguered parliamentary infantry in the centre.

For two hours the battle raged in the fields between Acton and Nantwich. The royalist forces, hampered by the narrow hedgerows and fields, unable to manoeuvre and unassisted by their own fleeing cavalry, surrendered to a man. At the end of the day, Byron had been driven back to Chester and over a thousand of his men had been taken prisoner.

That night Adam sat with his officers in the small parlour of the farmhouse that served as their billet for the night. They had counted their losses as two men dead and fifteen slightly wounded.

Like many of the men, Hewitson's wife, Mary, followed the drum, and she ensured they all had a hot meal and a dry bed. Now she sat beside the fire, mending her husband's shirt, torn by a pike in the affray. It presented a domestic scene at odds with the work of the day.

Adam sat apart from the others, staring into the depths of the fire, his fingers playing with the chain of the silver locket that hung from his neck. Only when he was alone did he take it off and dare open the catch and touch the lock of nut- brown hair that lay curled within it.

'Coulter.' Hewitson's voice roused him from his reverie and he looked up. 'Coulter,' Hewitson drew on his pipe and stared ruminatively at the ceiling. 'You did well today. We reckons as how you'll do.'

Chapter Twelve

PRESWOOD HALL, APRIL 1644

The spotted fever that had taken Simon did not spread to anyone else at Preswood, but over the winter a chill settled on Joan's chest. Her rattling cough echoed around the cold, cheerless house, casting a pall that even Bess and Robin's happiness could not relieve.

Spring brought the return of some warmth to the cold, damp countryside, but the first budding of the daffodils and primroses went unseen by Joan. Her world had become her bedchamber and Perdita knew that the balance of her friend's life was now measured in days not weeks.

She and Bess took it in turns to sit with Joan, occupying their time with reading to her or sewing quietly while she slept.

Joan occupied the best bedchamber in the house, and even though Geoffrey had been dead nearly two years, his presence still lingered, a unicorn's horn hung over the door and strange statues of sinuous dancers crowded the mantelpiece. Joan's unfinished portrait of Perdita and Simon stood propped on a table, a painful reminder of what might have been.

'Perdita.'

Perdita looked up from the account book she was working on.

Joan gestured to the portrait. 'Do you ever think about Adam? Do you wonder where he is and why he has sent me no word?'

Perdita turned her gaze on the portrait. Joan had completed the figure of Simon, but her own likeness remained little more than a ghost beneath the weight of Simon's painted hand. She remembered the likeness Adam had sketched of her and she swallowed back the tears.

Thoughts of Adam Coulter too often intruded on her waking and her dreams. Memories of the snatched moments of intimacy conflicted with guilt over Simon. If he had lived would she have ever learned to love him, the way she loved Adam Coulter or would Adam have always been there, those cold, grey eyes challenging her loyalty?

'I have had other matters to concern me,' she said.

Joan moved her gaze from the portrait to scan Perdita's face.

'Perdita, I have done Adam a great wrong and it is preying on my conscience. Do you have pen and ink? Please write for me.'

Perdita smoothed out a sheet of paper and dipped her pen in the ink.

Joan pulled herself up on the bolsters. 'Before I begin, you must swear to me you will never repeat what you hear to anyone, not even Bess?'

Puzzled, Perdita agreed and Joan sank back and closed her eyes.

My dearest Adam,

This is the hardest letter I have ever written but I know I am dying and I cannot face the Lord in the knowledge that I carry a secret to my grave that is your right to share.

When I was a girl of sixteen I was sent to Court to the household of the Queen. There I was seduced by a man who flattered me with poems and professions of love, but when I found I was with child he abandoned me, leaving me to the approbation of my parents. I was sent north to a distant kinswoman to give birth to the child of my shame. The child was left with this woman to take her name and I was returned, heartbroken at having to abandon my baby, to Marchants. When I contracted the rheumatic fever that was to plague me all my life, penance for my sin perhaps, I begged my parents to bring my child to me and to my surprise they relented and my brother, one of the very best of men, went to fetch the child. The child's father had been a boon companion of my brother and it was agreed between them that my brother would own the child as his. Thus you came to Marchants, Adam, as the bastard son of my brother to be brought up with your cousins as befitted you. How he prevailed upon his wife to accept the child, I still do not know, and she let her displeasure be known. All I, your mother, could do was watch over you through your childhood. Yours has not been an easy life and I was not always able to protect you from the wanton cruelties that a baseborn child must endure, but despite all you have suffered, you have grown into a man of whom I am proud.

I know the first question you would ask of me is to know the identity of your father and that I will not tell you. Nothing would be gained by that knowledge. He is long dead and those few who knew or suspected are also in heaven. My brother was as good a father to you as that man would ever have been and I will not take that from you. I have known great happiness with my beloved Geoffrey and that is my wish for you, to wed the one person you love. I will leave you well provided for. That distant kinswoman in the north country bequeathed me her entire estate at Strickland and it is yours. Her name was Ann Coulter, the name you bear. God watch over you as I will always do. Your ever-loving mother, Joan Clifford.

Joan lay back on the bolsters, her face grey with exhaustion. Perdita stared at the words on the page, trying to imagine what it meant to carry such a secret.

'How?' she began, 'How could you bear it?'

'I was there, Perdita. I saw my son grow into a man. That was all I asked. Do you think,' she grasped at her breath, 'do you think Adam will forgive me?'

Perdita looked at the dying woman, her mind turning over how she would react to such news. She would be angry, very angry, that this secret had been concealed from her.

'He will want to know about his father,' she said.

Joan turned her face away. 'His father is dead, Perdita.'

'Joan, this is a matter you should have rightly told him long before now,' she said. 'You had ample opportunity when he was here.'

'I intended to, but,' Joan swallowed, tears trailing from her eyes on to the embroidered covers. 'I could never... bring myself to do so. I suppose I am a coward, Perdita and now it is too late. It must be this way. When you see him, tell him that I have always loved him.'

'He knows that, Joan.'

'But not why... he needs to know why. Promise... promise me you will see he gets this letter. You must give it into his hand yourself. You must explain what I cannot.'

Perdita took the dying woman's hand in her own and made the promise.

Joan closed her eyes. Perdita sanded and sealed the letter and placed it safely in a secure place in her bedchamber. When she returned to Joan, she knew that this beloved woman would be dead by morning.

Joan's letter lay in a locked box in Perdita's bed chamber while Perdita pondered what to do about it. She had promised to deliver it into Adam's hand, but her own coward's soul quailed at the thought of seeing him, let alone being the bearer of such ill news. She hoped that he may come himself, riding past on some errand, but as the spring campaigning began their only regular visitor was

Robin and he had no news of Adam. She still delayed, using the weather as an excuse and justifying her failure to ride to Warwick on the muddy roads and beating spring rain.

It was well into May with the breath of fine weather taking away her last excuse, before Perdita set out for Warwick, riding pillion behind the faithful Ludovic. The last time she had taken this road had been on a quest to liberate Simon, and now it seemed to Perdita that the road would forever be associated with trouble and sadness.

She left the horse with Ludovic and once more walked the cobbled streets up to the castle, every step heavy with grief and with fear of how Adam would take the news. She had not dared let herself think about Adam, as if to do so would be unfaithful to Simon's memory. Simon, who had given her his heart, without condition, knowing she did not, could not, return that love.

At the end of the street, she stopped, looking up at the forbidding grey walls of the castle, formulating the words she would use to deliver the news of Joan's death, handing him the letter. She would not stay to see his face, feel his wrath, sense his grief. It was enough she knew the contents of the letter. She would hand him the letter and leave.

At the gate she asked to see Captain Coulter.

'Coulter?' the guard paused, scratching his unshaven chin. 'He's gone north, hasn't he, Sam?'

Sam nodded in agreement. 'Gone these five months past.'

Perdita stared from one to the other. 'Gone? But he sent no word...'

Why would he send word? He owed nobody at Preswood any particular favour, except perhaps Joan and, indeed a note to his aunt would have been politic. But this was war and courtesies such as that were not part of the day-to-day life of a soldier. Or did the truth lie deeper? Had he stayed away thinking her wed to Simon?

The two soldiers looked at her, undisguised curiosity in their gazes.

'Do you know where he has gone?' Perdita enquired.

The first soldier shrugged. 'Who's to say? I tell 'ee what. The Colonel be in. He'll be able to tell 'ee better than we.'

The governor of Warwick Castle, Colonel Purefoy, received her in the same elegant oak-panelled study last occupied by Adam. She remembered the concern in his eyes, his swift, sure hands, guiding her to a chair. His touch.

'Mistress Gray.' The Colonel's brisk tone returned her to the present. 'What business do you have with me?'

'My business is with Adam Coulter. Your men tell me he has gone north.'

Purefoy nodded. 'At his request, he left in the new year to join Fairfax. It seemed a sensible decision. He was not one for garrison life.' The colonel pursed his lips as if remembering some incident that had illustrated Adam's unsuitability to remain at the castle. 'Do you mind me asking, what's your business with him?'

Something in the flick of his eyebrow made Perdita wonder if Purefoy suspected that she had come to foist an unwanted pregnancy upon Adam.

'I am his kinswoman,' Perdita extended their relationship, 'and I am, unhappily, the bearer of sad news concerning the death of a close member of his family.'

Purefoy almost looked disappointed. He shook his head. 'Death is all around us, is it not, Mistress Gray? It seems to me my task is forever dealing with the death of somebody's son or brother or father. However, if you wish to send on a letter, I have a supply convoy for the north leaving in the morning. The letter can be entrusted to Captain Burns.'

Perdita bit her lip, conscious that her disappointment must seem ill disguised. 'It is not a matter I can entrust to someone else, Colonel.'

Purefoy spread his hands. 'There it is, Mistress Gray. I am afraid Coulter is unlikely to return to Warwick and where exactly he is now, I am unable to say. Except that when last I heard news from the north, Fairfax was laying siege to York. The offer stands if you wish to send a missive with Captain Burns, ensure it is in his hands at first light tomorrow.'

Perdita took her leave of Colonel Purefoy and trudged back to the inn where Ludovic waited.

'He's not here, Ludovic. He's gone north to be with Fairfax. I suppose there is nothing I can do but wait until he comes south again.'

Ludovic looked at her. 'Forgive my speaking plain, Mistress Gray. What is there to hold you here? Go with the supply wagons yourself.'

Perdita stared at him. 'I can't leave Bess,' she said.

Ludovic shrugged. 'Mistress Clifford has Lieutenant Marchant and I to watch over her. You will be safe enough with the supply train,' Ludovic said. 'It would simply be a matter of delivering the letter and returning back with it. You will only be gone a short while.'

Perdita bit her lip as her mind worked through Ludovic's suggestion. Did she dare? The worse that could happen was that Adam would hear her news and politely put her on the next transport south. At best? Perdita glanced up at the big man. Ludovic knew her better than she knew herself; nothing tied her to Warwickshire, at least nothing that couldn't spare her for a few weeks.

'Dare I?' she asked aloud.

'You know the answer to that question, Mistress Gray,' Ludovic said. 'Take a room for the night and pen a note to Mistress Clifford. I will take it and return with some coin and baggage for you.'

'It's a two hour ride.'

Ludovic shrugged. 'I will stay and see you safely bestowed on the convoy in the morning.'

Perdita begged a pen and paper from the landlord of the inn and wrote a short note to Bess, explaining that Joan had entrusted the letter for her to deliver personally and she had no choice but to go north to try and find Adam and fulfil her promise to Joan. All being well, she would return within the month.

Alone in the bedchamber of the inn, Perdita watched Ludovic ride away and pondered the folly of the quest she was about to undertake.

Clutching a bundle containing a clean gown, a change of linen and her comb, a blanket and some food, packed by Bess along with a note expressing her love and concern and praying that Perdita return soon and safely, Perdita strode down the streets to find the supply wagons assembling in the field below the castle.

Ludovic had also passed on a bag of coins and a small, fiendishly sharp knife. 'For food,' he had said, but the warning gaze he fixed on her told her it served a second purpose. Her own protection.

Amidst the scurrying figures, the cursing wagoners and bored soldiers, she sought out the harassed young officer whose task it was to organise the convoy. He had just despatched two burly troopers to deal with two women who were brawling, apparently over possession of a piece of cloth.

'Captain Burns?'

With one eye still on the fracas, he half-turned toward her. 'Mistress?'

'Colonel Purefoy has granted me permission to join your

convoy.' While not exactly the truth, she saw no point in bothering Purefoy on such a trivial matter.

He brought his full attention to her. Looking her up and down, no doubt wondering if she was another doxy anxious to follow the soldiers. His sandy eyebrows rose as he scanned her from her well-polished shoe to the white linen coif beneath a wide brimmed hat.

'If Purefoy has granted you permission then I cannot stop you. Do you mind me asking what your business is that takes you north?'

Perdita saw no reason to lie and, raising her voice over a tremendous cheer from the crowd which had gathered to watch the two brawling women, she said, 'I am seeking Captain Adam Coulter.'

But the attention of the young man had swung back to the brawl. Two of his troopers had intervened, physically picking up the two spatting women.

'I beg your pardon, did you say, Coulter?' He looked back at her. 'Good heavens Mistress Coulter! I had no idea that you would be joining us or even...'

He had plainly misheard her and Perdita opened her mouth to refute the notion that she was Adam Coulter's wife, but the young man had already turned and walked away.

'Please follow me, Mistress Coulter. I will see what we can offer in the way of some small comfort.'

Perdita hurried after him, desperate to correct the misunderstanding. 'Please Captain, I...'

But his stride was too long and she could not make herself heard above the noise of the baggage train moving off. Towards the rear, a wagon with three women lumbered past. The officer stopped it.

'Here, mistress. There is room for one more. You there, Peg, make room for Mistress Coulter. She will be travelling with us to the north.' He bowed. 'I'll leave you with these ladies, and if you are free for dinner tonight, I hope you will join me. I shall ensure that there is suitable accommodation found for you.'

He turned and strode away, calling for his horse.

A red-haired woman leaned out of the wagon, holding out her hand.

'Come aboard, lass.'

Perdita threw her baggage into the wagon and grasped the woman's hand, landing ungracefully on the sacks of grain.

'Well, well. It looks like we've a lady here!' the red-haired woman remarked to her companions as Perdita settled herself into a corner.

Perdita looked around at her travelling companions, apart from the large red-head, there was a slim dark-haired girl in scarlet petticoats and a sensible matronly woman with a sallow, wrinkled face.

Peg leaned forward. 'And what business do you have in the north?'

'I...I'm seeking Adam Coulter. I've been told he left the Warwick garrison in January.'

'You his wife? I heard Burns call you Mistress Coulter,' the matronly woman said.

The seed of the lie had been sown. What did it matter if these people thought her Adam's wife? It gave credence to her tale. Perdita nodded and in that moment she became Adam Coulter's wife in the eyes of her three companions.

If she had said she was the wife of King Charles himself, she could not have produced a more shocked response. All three women stared at her open-mouthed.

'Adam Coulter has a wife?' the girl in the scarlet gown said at last.

Perdita met the girl's astonished gaze. 'You know my husband?'

Peg nodded and looked around at the other. 'Aye, we know your 'usband well.'

Red skirts winked. 'There are several women who can say that,'

Appalled by the implication, Perdita stared at the women in horror, provoking a laugh.

'No need to look like that, mistress,' Peg said. 'You can be assured that while many of us may have fancied a night or two in Adam Coulter's bed, none to my knowledge ever made it there. Didn't I say, Hetty, that he was a faithful one?'

'Aye, and a waste of his fine eyes, I did say.'

''Twas not his eyes I was thinking of.' Red skirts gave her companions a lascivious grin. 'So what's he like in bed, love?'

Perdita swallowed, saved from a response by a peal of laughter from the woman.

'You're right, Peg. We've got a real lady here.'

The matronly woman, Hetty, regarded her through narrow eyes. 'So what brings you to this pass, Mistress Coulter? The soldiering life is no place for a lady such as yourself. What's your business with him?'

'My business is just that, my business,' Perdita snapped.

The woman shrugged and turned to the other two, ignoring Perdita who settled herself as comfortably as she could and prepared herself for a long, uncomfortable journey. She had the uneasy feeling that she knew very little of the man whose wife she now professed to be. She'd been a fool to let the misunderstanding go unchallenged, to have allowed a myth to perpetuate, but now it seemed she had to live with it.

Captain Burns remained polite and deferential, even procuring a small, hardy pony for her to ride in preference to the wagons. The convoy made a slow, ponderous journey north. The days stretching into a second week before Burns rode up to her one morning.

'Mistress,' he said. 'My orders are only to go as far as Leeds. You must make the rest of the way by yourself.'

Perdita's heart skipped a beat. Leeds was still miles short of York, if that's where Adam could be found.

'How am I to find him?'

Burns looked at her and shrugged. He had the grace to look concerned. He had taken very good care of her and they had enjoyed several evening meals together.

He shook his head. 'Those are my orders. Perhaps I can spare a man to take you on to the next garrison. After that you must find your own way.'

Relief flooded Perdita. 'Thank you, Captain. That will be fine. I am sure to find someone who will take me further.'

'I hope you find Coulter without too much trouble.' The captain's doubtful frown belied his smile. He stared off into the distance before bringing his gaze back to her, all trace of humour gone from his eyes.

'Forgive me speaking plain, mistress, but once your business with your husband is done, I would suggest you turn for home. It is no gentle war we are fighting any more, but harsh and bloody. No place for you. I'll be returning to Warwick by week's end. If you can return before I leave, I will see you safely home.'

'Thank you, Captain,' Perdita replied, her heart warmed by the offer. 'You're not the first to warn me of the dangers. Please do not trouble yourself about me.'

'Very well, mistress.' He still looked troubled as he bowed from the saddle, before turning his horse and cantering away.

At Leeds the next day a dour corporal presented himself. He said little to Perdita but every inch of his body was stiff with indignation. Evidently, he did not appreciate being nursemaid to a woman.

They rode in silence and toward evening encountered a body of infantry. The corporal rode up to the officer at their head and saluted sharply. They conducted a conversation out of Perdita's earshot and she sat her plump little mare uncomfortably aware of the gesturing and sharp glances in her direction. Satisfied, the corporal turned and trotted back to her.

'I'll leave you with these men,' he said. 'They're Lord Fairfax's men and they can take you closer to York. Chances are your man's thereabouts.'

'Thank you for your help, Corporal,' Perdita said to the man's back as he gratefully put his spurs to his horse to return to Leeds. The officer fell in beside her.

'Coulter? Is he with Black Tom?'

Perdita frowned. 'If that's what they call Sir Thomas Fairfax?'

The man grinned. 'It is, mistress. Coulter? Aye, I recall the name. He was with us at Nantwich, was he not, Sergeant?'

The sergeant who rode beside him nodded. 'Aye, fought like the devil at Nantwich from what I hear tell. He'll be outside York with Black Tom's men.'

'You're welcome to ride with us, lady, and we can take you as far as our encampment. Someone else can take you on from there.'

It had begun to rain as she jogged along behind the soldiers. Never having been a rider, she felt every muscle in her body. So far from home, in the company of these rough men, Perdita admitted to herself that she was alone and very afraid.

For the next two days, she passed from camp to camp in her efforts to find Adam. At least the parliamentary forces of the north were largely in one area, hunkered down staring at the walls of York. It made the distances to be travelled easier but food and beds were scarce and the rain persisted. Her personal resources were sadly dissipated. She seemed to be permanently wet and for the last couple of days her head throbbed as if a thousand blacksmiths worked at it.

It seemed forever before she at last encountered someone who knew that Major Coulter could be found at Fulford, a little village a few miles south of York. Perdita's thanks were heartfelt. With no one to escort her, she rode the last few miles alone in the drizzling rain, her body craving nothing more than a soft bed and oblivion.

Outside Fulford she was stopped by soldiers and once more she had to explain that she sought Major Coulter, that she had family business with him. They let her through without further question, directing her to the inn which stood on the main road, a comfortable stone building bearing the sign of the Moor's Head.

She left her horse in the care of the ostler and dragged her leaden feet into the inn. A neat maid directed her to a small parlour where three men sat smoking their pipes and talking amongst themselves. She hesitated in the door and they leaped to their feet on seeing her. A wave of disappointment swept over her when she saw that Adam was not amongst them.

'I'm sorry to disturb you,' she said, their curious faces wavering before her eyes, 'I'm seeking Major Coulter. I'm told he lodges here.'

The older of the men, a solid man with a hard face, replied in a heavy Yorkshire brogue that in Perdita's befuddled state she could barely decipher.

'I'm sorry, Mistress. Ye've just missed him. He's gone to Fairfax and we don't expect him back much before tomorrow or't next day.'

Betraying tears pricked the back of Perdita's throat. She had come so far only to have missed him?

'But I must see him.'

The officer looked at her with narrowed eyes. 'May I ask what it concerns?'

She hesitated, but after the two weeks on the road the lie came quickly to her tongue, 'I am his wife. I will wait for his return.'

Three stunned faces stared back at her for a long moment before the older officer cleared his throat. 'His wife, is it? I'll get the landlord to show 'ee to his room.'

Relief flooded over her. If it meant a wait, she had at least found Adam.

The headache had been steadily growing like a band around her head and she could barely keep her eyes open.

'Thank you, I...' She stumbled into the room, groping for a chair like a drunken man.

'Are ye quite well, mistress?' One of the younger men caught her arm, guiding her into a chair.

'No,' she admitted and added, 'in fact I think I am going to be sick.'

A bowl was thrust into her hands and to her shame she was violently ill. Through her misery she could hear the firm voice of the Yorkshireman.

'The lass has a fever. You, Williams, fetch my wife. Brown, help me take her up to the major's room.'

Too weak and too sick to protest, Perdita felt herself lifted like a child and carried up the stairs. They laid her on a bed and she turned her face gratefully towards the clean, linen bolster while the world swam and lurched about her.

'Now then what's to be done with thee?' A woman's voice this time, laced with the same thick Yorkshire brogue as her rescuer.

'Just a little tired,' Perdita said.

A firm, cool, hand pressed on her forehead. 'Ye've a fever and no doubt of that. Now sit up.'

As limp as a rag doll, Perdita allowed herself to be hauled into a sitting position and, despite her feeble protests, her clothes were swiftly removed and a cool, clean shift slipped over her head. The movement caused the nausea to rise and she was ill again, a bowl firmly held under her chin. Her nurse laid her back on the bed, pulled the bed clothes up and laid a cold cloth on her forehead.

'Now ye sleep, lass. I'll sit by ye and if ye've a yen to be ill again, just you say.'

'So tired.' Perdita's eyes closed and her world became one of demons who mocked and taunted her from the bed hangings. Simon came and stood beside her. She reached out for him, only to feel him melt away at her touch with a slow, sad smile.

'Ye're awake then?'

Perdita turned her head and opened her eyes to see a small, red-faced woman standing over her. The woman placed a hand on her forehead.

'Cool too. That's good. Now drink this.'

Perdita swallowed. Her head and body no longer ached and the world no longer lurched and swam but her mouth tasted like the vats of hell and she doubted she had the strength to raise her head.

The woman slipped her arm under Perdita's shoulders and helped her to sit up, placing a mug to her lips.

'Let's see if ye can hold it down.'

Perdita drank the thin gruel and the woman set her back on the bolster.

'How long have I been here?' Perdita asked.

'This is the second day,' the woman replied, busying herself with plumping the bolster and smoothing down the bed clothes.

Perdita looked around the room, probably one of the best rooms the inn provided. The bed was comfortable and a fire burned in the hearth.

Adam's room. Of its occupant, she saw little evidence, save a wooden chest on which a pair of well-polished shoes stood, a pile of papers, a couple of books and a pen stand on the table. She closed her eyes and took a deep breath, seeking some scent of him but all she could smell was dust and beeswax polish mingled with the rank smell of sickness.

'Is Adam Coulter returned?' Perdita forced herself to ask.

The woman shook her head. 'Not yet. Obadiah expects him today.' She paused and smiled. 'Ye're probably wondering whom I am. Captain Obadiah Hewitson is my husband. I'm Mary Hewitson.'

Perdita expected that Obadiah Hewitson was the solid, unremarkable officer she had first encountered downstairs and in whose arms she had been so violently ill.

'Thank you for your kindness, Mistress Hewitson. Both of you.'

She shrugged. 'Praise be to God for your swift recovery. I must confess, Mistress Coulter, ye caused me no small concern. I feared ye may be carrying plague.'

Perdita started at the use of the stolen name. When Adam returned, she would be unmasked and she feared his wrath as much as the shame of the pretence.

'Have ye come a long way?' Mary enquired.

'Warwickshire.'

The woman put her hands on her hips and regarded her. 'And why, pray, have ye trekked half way across England, risking life and limb in these perilous times?'

'I have family business with him.'

Mary narrowed her eyes. 'Is it ill news?'

Perdita nodded. 'The worst news.' To forestall what she knew would be the next question, she added, 'It is for his ears only.'

'Well lass, I doubt that ye'd have risked coming here if it were good news,' Mary remarked. 'I must leave you. There's a bowl beside the bed, should you have need of it but I think the worst has passed.' She briskly tucked in the sheets around Perdita. 'Now sleep. Ye'll need yer strength for when yer husband returns.'

The door clicked shut behind her good Samaritan and Perdita let out a breath. In the days since she had left Warwick, she had rehearsed her meeting with Adam and what she would say. Flat on her back, reeking of recent illness, was not part of the plan but there was precious little she could do about it. Obedient to Mary

Hewitson's instructions she let herself drift into a peaceful, untroubled sleep.

Adam slid off his horse's back, tossing the reins to the inn's ostler. Pulling off his gauntlets he strode into the inn.

'Hewitson!'

His second-in-command rose from his chair by the hearth, knocking the ash from his pipe. Adam threw his gauntlets on to the table, followed by his hat.

'What news, sir?' Hewitson enquired.

The tapster stood at Adam's elbow with a mug of ale which Adam quaffed without drawing breath, setting the empty mug on the table.

'Rupert is marching on us to relieve York,' he said at last. 'Black Tom reckons he'll join battle with us in the next week.'

Hewitson's eyebrows raised slightly, the only sign of emotion on his dour face. They both knew what that meant. Any battle fought with Rupert would decide who controlled the north.

'And what does Black Tom say?'

Adam shrugged. 'Fairfax's confident and he has good men beside him. This time the ground will be of our choosing.' He huffed out a breath and shrugged his stiff shoulders. 'That's why it's taken so damn long. I've been on reconnaissance.'

'And the ground, sir?'

'Do you know the villages of Long Marston and Tockwith?'

Hewitson inclined his head. 'Aye, good flat land.'

Adam shrugged. 'We'll see.' He rubbed his leg. Denzil's pistol ball had left the legacy of a nagging ache in cold and damp weather. 'I for one intend a good night's sleep. I'll see you in the morning, Hewitson.'

'Aye sir.' Hewitson picked his pipe up again, fumbling for his tobacco pouch as Adam scooped up gloves and hat.

As Adam turned towards the door, Hewitson said, 'There's one thing, Coulter...'

Adam turned back. 'That is?'

Hewitson pulled his pipe from his mouth and pointed at the ceiling with the stem. 'Your wife's upstairs. She's been right poorly but Mary's seen to her and she's on the mend.'

'My wife?' Adam stared at the man.

A frown creased Hewitson's brow. 'Aye, pretty lass with brown hair. Been halfway round the country trying to find you.'

Adam swallowed. 'My wife?' he repeated.

'Aye, sir, your wife.' Hewitson frowned with puzzled patience.

Adam swore under his breath and turned for the stairs. He took the steps two at a time, pausing outside the door to his chamber to gather his strength to deal with whatever doxy was passing herself off as his wife.

He took a breath and flung open the door.

'What in God's name is going on here?' he demanded.

The bedclothes stirred and in the fading light, a woman sat up, pushing her disordered hair away from her eyes.

'Adam, at last.'

Adam blinked a couple of times as his eyes became accustomed to the gloom and he recognised the occupant of his bed.

He leaned back against the door frame, closing the door behind him and ran a hand over his eyes. He must be more tired than he realised.

'Perdita! That fool Hewitson told me my wife was upstairs. I thought...' he shrugged. He had thought one of the camp followers had inveigled her way past Hewitson. Not Perdita Gray.

She shook her head. 'Don't blame him, Adam. It's my mistake, a stupid misunderstanding I should have corrected but now it's too late. They think I'm your wife.'

163

Adam straightened and walked over to the bed. Looking down into her pale, drawn face, he realised with a jolt that she had indeed been ill. The brown eyes that looked back at him, filled with apprehension, were huge and luminous in the beautiful face.

He ran a finger down her cheek, tilting her chin to the fading light. Beneath his touch she shivered, clutching at the bed clothes.

'Hewitson said you've been ill?'

'Just a fever. I've been well looked after, Adam.'

Her thin shift had slipped down revealing a soft white shoulder and a tantalising glimpse of what lay beneath. Adam took a breath and turned away from her, tossing his gauntlets and hat on to the table.

He turned back to face her. He knew he should be angry with her but what woman traipsed halfway across England, passing herself off as his wife? None, unless they had a very good reason.

'So, Mistress Gray, are you going to tell me the reason for this subterfuge?'

She swallowed. 'Believe me, I would not have come, but I made a promise.' She lowered her head, covering her eyes with her hand as her shoulders rose and fell.

Adam crossed to bed and sat down beside her. He raised his hand, intending to draw her to him, brush that messy hair from her eyes and kiss the tears away.

He took a breath and let his hand fall, reminding himself that she was another's wife.

'Am I right in assuming you bring me ill news?'

Perdita nodded and sniffed, wiping the tears with the back of her hand. 'The worst. I promised Joan...'

'Joan?' The breath left his body. It could only be Joan. No one else in his accursed family would warrant such an undertaking by this woman.

She looked up at him, her eyes still brimming with tears. 'She died of the lung fever in April.' She took his hand, forcing him to look at her. 'I have a letter for you, Adam.' She swallowed, her fingers tightening on his. 'I promised to deliver it to your hand, so I went to Warwick but they told me you had come north so I had no choice. I had to come.'

Adam extricated his hand and stood up. 'It was foolish promise, Perdita.' He knew his tone sounded harsh, but she evidently did not comprehend the risks to a beautiful woman travelling alone through a country torn by war.

Her mouth tightened. 'Nevertheless, it was a promise, Adam.'

'Where is this letter?'

Perdita gestured to a leather bag that stood on the chest at the foot of the bed beside his shoes. 'It's in there.'

Adam unbuckled the bag and drew out the crumpled and stained parchment. A testimony to the travails Perdita had endured to bring it to his hand.

He glanced at the superscription and cast Perdita a suspicious glance. 'This is not Joan's writing.'

'It's mine,' Perdita said. 'She dictated it to me.'

'So you know what it contains?'

She nodded.

He turned away from her and crossed to the window to catch the last of the light as he broke the seal, conscious that she watched him. When he had read Joan's last words to him he did not move but stood staring down at the words on the page. Everything he had believed and understood about himself and his place in the world tilted on its edge, slid and shattered at his feet.

He let his hand fall, crumpling the letter in his grip. He hurled the balled letter at the wall, crossed to the table and snatched up his hat and gloves.

'Where are you going?' Perdita threw back the covers and put her feet to the floor but he did not see her. All he could think about was the woman he should have called his mother. Too late now. Too late.

'There's an enemy resupply column not twenty miles from here. We'll hit it tonight.'

'Adam!'

He heard her call his name and it cut like a knife to his heart as he slammed the door behind him.

The whole room shuddered as the door crashed shut. Perdita sat on the edge of the bed and lowered her face to her hands. Beyond the door his footsteps echoed on the stairs as he shouted for his men.

With an effort she stood up, the floor beneath her feet tossing as she crept along the length of the bed. Cursing the weakness of her recent illness and with tears welling in her eyes, she lurched to the window.

In the courtyard the soldiers gathered, some still saddling their horses. Adam sat astride Robin's horse, his face shadowed by the heavy pot helmet he wore.

She leaned against the wall and laid her hand on the diamond panes of the window, feeling the cool glass beneath her fingers.

'Adam. God go with you,' she whispered as the tears slid down her face.

As she watched, he wheeled his horse and was gone, his men clattering after him.

'And what do you think you're doing?' Mary Hewitson stood in the doorway, holding a candle in one hand and a bowl in the other. 'Back into bed at once, young lady.'

Grateful for the shadows that hid her face and obedient to Mary's command, Perdita groped her way back to the bed.

Mary stood over her patient with her hands on her hips. 'I

don't know what it was you said to our commander but he came down those stairs with the very devil in him.'

Perdita looked away. 'It was ill news.'

Mary sniffed, 'Aye well, it's none of my business, although if his black humour kills my 'usband it'll be me he will be reckoning with.'

Perdita looked up at her wanting to reassure her but not finding the words. Adam Coulter had never seemed like a reckless man but she had never seen the wild grief in his eyes before. Tonight he could be capable of anything.

'Hope you're hungry.'

Mary passed her the bowl and pulled up a chair. Perdita obediently tucked into the fragrant stew. It tasted good and she realised for the first time in weeks she was hungry.

'Why did you decide to follow the drum?' Perdita asked to change the subject.

Mary shrugged. 'Obadiah and I hail from 't dales. He went a soldiering when the old Lord Fairfax went to't Low Countries and I went with him then. Ten years I've been a soldier's wife, bearing my children in barns or by't side of the road and I'd not exchange it for that of a farmer's wife.'

Perdita looked at the woman with new eyes, trying to imagine the life of a camp follower and failing dismally.

'Where are your children now?'

'Four children I've borne. Two've died and t'others live with my sister in Whitby. For all I'd follow Obadiah to the end of the world and back, I'd not have my children along with me.'

'You must miss them.'

Mary's face softened. 'Aye of course I do, but I sleep better for knowing they're as safe as can be. Have ye children, Mistress Coulter?'

Perdita shook her head.

Mary Hewitson nodded. 'Ye're both young. There's time. I take it you've nought been married long?'

It took Perdita a moment to realise she referred to Adam and the heat rose in her cheeks. For both their sakes, she had to extricate herself from this mess in which she had landed them.

She ignored the question. 'I'll be leaving in the morning.'

Mary Hewitson raised an eyebrow. 'Oh will ye now, and you just out of your sick bed? Anyway enough chatter, lass. You need your sleep and I, mine. Drink this. It will help you sleep.'

Obediently Perdita took the draught Mary proffered and lay down, allowing herself to drift into a deep, black dreamless hole where she did not have to tell the man she loved that the woman he had known all his life as his aunt, was his mother.

The clatter of horses' hooves and the sound of men's voices woke Perdita as the first streaks of dawn began to light the sky.

Please let that be Adam, she prayed.

She put a tentative foot to the floor and, relieved to find it stayed solid and unmoving, she padded over to the window. The courtyard had filled with soldiers. Adam's patrol had returned, and from the wagons that now lined the street, it seemed that his aim to intercept the enemy supply column had met with some success.

Obadiah Hewitson, helmetless, hands on hips, his face grimed and grey with exhaustion, stood in the centre of the courtyard, issuing orders. She scanned the faces but could not see Adam. Her heart lurched. She had to know if he had returned. She could not wait here like a pallid milksop.

A pitcher and bowl stood on the table and Perdita poured some water into the bowl and washed herself as thoroughly as the meagre circumstances allowed. She found her gown, cleaned and pressed, neatly folded on the chair and gave a silent thanks to Mary Hewitson. After she had fought her dull, lifeless hair into some semblance of order, stuffing it beneath a coif, she went downstairs where she found Mary Hewitson alone in the inn parlour.

Mary pushed a plate of porridge across the table to Perdita. 'You look better today. Nothing like a good night's sleep to allow God's healing I always say.'

'No small thanks to you,' Perdita acknowledged.

'Aye well. It's only what any poor Christian would do.' Mary sniffed and wiped her hands on her apron.

'Adam?' Perdita asked.

Mary looked up sharply. 'He's all right, lass. Ridden on to report to Black Tom, he has. He'll be back later.'

Perdita looked down at the bowl of congealing oats, hoping that Mary would not notice the relief that flooded through her.

Mary nodded at the bowl. 'You eat now. If ye're up to it, we've woman's work to do.'

'What sort of work?'

Mary's lips narrowed. 'Ye're a camp follower now, Mistress Coulter, and there's wounded to tend to. Ye're not given to faints and swooning at't sight of blood are ye?'

Perdita shook her head. 'Not normally.'

As soon as both women had eaten, Perdita donned an apron, took off her collar and cuffs, and picking up a basket of bandages Mary thrust at her, followed her new friend across the road to the church where the wounded had been taken.

The church had become an infirmary and the wounded were laid on straw around the walls. Perdita's nose curled at the smell and her barely-cured stomach lurched. She took a breath and steeled her nerve. She could not let sensibilities overcome her when there was work to be done and she had done this work before.

Adam had paid a price for taking the supply train but it could have been worse. Three men were dead and eight wounded, with three of those close to death.

Perdita knelt beside a trooper who had a bad blow to the head and was raving in a delirium. Someone had tied a rough bandage around the hideous wound and he fought her efforts to try and redress the wound.

The trooper sat up wide eyed. 'We mun get away! They follow us.'

'You're safe now. Be still.' It came as a command, brisk and harsh but it had its effect.

At the sound of Adam's voice, the man quieted in Perdita's hands.

Adam knelt beside Perdita and with firm but gentle hands on the man's shoulder, they laid him back on the rough bed. 'Let this good woman see to that wound, Oldham.'

The man turned his wide-eyed stare on to his commander's face. 'Are they gone?' the man asked.

'They're gone,' Adam replied.

The trooper, mollified, closed his eyes.

Adam did not move as Perdita finished her task without further resistance.

'What was he talking about?' she asked.

Adam shrugged. 'Any number of incidents. Before I took command of this company they had been through hell. The north was all but lost.'

'And now?'

'Rupert is even now marching to relieve York and the fate of the north will be decided once and for all.'

'It will come to battle?'

'Inevitably.'

Adam stood up with a grunt, ruefully rubbing his leg. He held out his hand and helped her up.

'Your leg still bothers you?' Perdita asked.

He shook his head. 'My leg's fine. I've been on horseback the better part of three days. I'm just tired.' He looked around the church. 'And my men here are in considerably more need of your hands than I am.'

He turned away and limped down the row of men. Perdita watched as he moved from one man to another, talking to them and reassuring them as he had done after the battle of Edgehill. Perdita watched his soldiers' faces and the eyes that followed his progress. For a foreigner from the south, it seemed to her that Adam Coulter had done much to win the respect of his men.

'Well he seems in a might better humour this day.' Mary joined Perdita and they stood together as Adam left the church. 'There were some who felt my Obadiah should have been promoted but Coulter proved himself at Nantwich and he's earned his office. His men are never short of rations or equipment like some we could name.' She glanced at Perdita. 'For all of that, we know him no better now than we did when he first came to us. We had no notion he'd a wife.'

'I always said that what the major needed was someone to warm his bed at night.'

Perdita turned to see one of the women who had been tending the wounded, a young, pretty and extremely curvaceous girl. Her gown seemed a little small for her and flesh spilled from the top of her bodice in a decidedly unladylike and definitely ungodly fashion.

'You be thankful. Ye've a good man in your husband, Peggy Brown,' Mary scolded.

The girl pouted. 'Who wants a good man? I think someone like the major would prove much better sport between the sheets than my Lemuel.'

'Down on your knees and pray.' Mary sounded genuinely shocked. 'The major is a married man. This 'ere's his wife.'

'I thought that was what you said.' The girl shot Perdita a glance, her lower lip pouting as she said with lowered eyes, 'I apologise for speaking out of turn, Mistress Coulter.' Her glance flashed back. 'You must be an angel to hold him in such a thrall. There's few men can resist what I have to offer.' With that the girl flounced off, her hips swaying as she walked.

'Mistress Coulter, you pay no mind to Peg. For all her talk she has a good man in Lemuel and she knows it.'

Perdita smiled. 'She would not be the first,' she said, remembering the women from Warwick.

At the end of a long day Perdita and Mary returned to the inn. Desperate to wash and change her gown, at the door to Adam's bedchamber Perdita hesitated. Did she knock or just walk in? What would a wife do?

She knocked and entered.

Adam had been asleep, still fully dressed, although his helmet, gauntlets and heavy breast and back plate lay stacked on the floor at the end of the bed. As the door clicked shut behind Perdita, he rolled over and sat up, shaking his head.

'Perdita, what are you...?' He paused. 'Oh... I forgot you're my wife and therefore entitled to be here.'

Perdita held out her stained skirts. 'I need to change.'

Did she detect the ghost of a smile, twitching the corners of his mouth as he said, 'That can wait a minute or two. We must talk before this matter gets any more out of hand.'

Perdita sat in a chair beside the table and waited while Adam rose from the bed and padded in his stockinged feet across to the window. He braced his arms against the casement and stood staring out into the bustling courtyard.

'What am I to do with you?' he said at last.

'I know I have to go back to Warwickshire,' she said. 'I will leave in the morning.'

He turned to face her. 'You're barely out of your sick bed. Besides I can't afford anyone to escort you.'

'I can—'

'No, you can't!' He ran a hand through his hair and paced the room. 'God's death, Simon Clifford must have been mad to let you even attempt this journey.'

'Simon?' She stared up at him.

Of course, he didn't know? How could he know?'

'Adam,' she swallowed, 'Simon is dead.'

He stared at her. 'Dead?'

'You know he was ill when you freed him from Warwick Castle. He'd contracted the spotted fever and died on the day we were to be wed.'

Adam stopped his pacing and stood in front of her, all anger and irritation gone from his face to be replaced with profound grief.

'Simon is dead? Perdita. I'm sorry. He was a good man. I liked him.' He paused. 'I counted him a friend and there are few in this world I can count in that number.'

Perdita bit her lip to stop the tears. 'He was too good to me, and, yes, I miss him.' She looked away, dashing at the tears that spilled too easily these days. 'And then to lose Joan. Grief heaped on grief, Adam.'

The pain welled up in her and she buried her face in her hands.

'Perdita.' Her name came on an exhaled breath as he knelt before her and took her in his arms.

She leaned her head against the reassuring solidity of his jacket and he stroked her hair and hushed her like a child. When her grief had subsided, he sat back on his heels and put his hand to her face, ineffectually wiping the tears away with his thumb

'You're exhausted, Perdita.'

She sniffed. 'It's been a hard winter,' she said. 'So much death.'

'For both of us.' He cupped her face in his hand and smiled. 'I owe you an apology for my behaviour last night.'

She shook her head. 'I cannot even begin to imagine what a shock it must have been to read Joan's words.'

'But you didn't deserve to take the blame.'

He rose to his feet and picked up a paper from the table. Perdita recognised Joan's letter, now much crumpled. He scanned the page and shook his head.

'For over thirty years I've been to the world, and to myself, the bastard son of Lord Marchant and a dead woman called Ann Coulter. I had two half-brothers, at least one of whom would see me dead, and an aunt,' he swallowed, 'an aunt who was as close as any mother could have been.' He tapped the page. 'In a few short words she took all that from me, leaving me only with questions that no one can now answer.' He tossed the paper back on the table. 'Now what do I do, Perdita Gray?'

She shook her head. 'I don't know.'

He frowned. 'Why couldn't she tell me this when we had the opportunity, when I could have asked her?'

'Probably for exactly that reason, Adam. She couldn't face your anger or your questions.'

He strode back to the window, and stood for a long moment looking out into the gloaming.

'Whatever my past, it must wait. In the meantime, I have the more immediate problem of Rupert's imminent arrival at the gates of York and,' he turned to look at her again, the ghost of a smile tugging at his mouth, 'a hitherto unknown wife who has inconveniently landed upon me.'

Perdita stood up and looked around the comfortable room. 'Maybe I could just stay here until matters settle.'

He shook his head. 'I can't leave you in an inn in Fulford. Nowhere is safe.' He paced the floor again before coming to stop in front of her. He laid his hands on her shoulders, forcing her to look up at him. She expected to see anger in their grey depths but when he spoke it was without rancour. 'God's death, Perdita. I don't need this but it seems I have no choice but to carry on your charade.'

Perdita looked up at him. 'I'm sorry, Adam. It truly began as a misunderstanding that I could not remedy.'

He shook his head and gave a hollow laugh. 'These are godly people. They are not going to understand or countenance this arrangement if they were to know the truth. You can take the bed. I'll sleep on the floor.' When she protested, he said, 'It's not the first time in my life I've had hard boards for a mattress. Now, *Mistress Coulter*, we had best make ourselves respectable. My officers will be expecting us to join them for dinner.'

Perdita had retired early to bed, swaying on her feet with exhaustion, and she did not stir as Adam returned to the chamber. He stood for a long moment looking down at her. She lay curled on her side, her hair spread out on the bolsters. By the light of the candle, all the care had gone from the face and his heart ached at the sight of her. It would be so easy to slip into the bed beside her and take her in his arms. The knowledge she had never become Simon Clifford's wife did not make her his. He had to win her love and in the circumstances neither of them needed, or had the time for, the niceties of courtship.

The thought of even sleeping on the floor in the same bedchamber as Perdita Gray provoked a reaction in him that made the alternative of the oak settle in the parlour look like the safer course of action.

Trying to make as little noise as possible, he retrieved a blanket and bolster and made a bed for himself in the parlour, which was where his general's galloper, Richard Ashley found him in the morning with the news that Rupert was on the move and Fairfax wanted all his officers to assemble.

He left a note for Perdita and, taking Hewitson, rode to the

General's headquarters. They did not return until long past night-fall and, rather than disturb Perdita, Adam chose to pass another night in the parlour, which raised a questioning eyebrow from his second in command.

'She needs her sleep,' he mumbled in excuse.

And so do I, he could have added.

But he was on the march in the morning and he had to pack his few belongings and be ready to leave by daybreak. Long before first light, he returned to the bedchamber and woke her. She sat up in bed.

'Where did you sleep these last two nights?' she asked.

'Downstairs. You need to be up and dressed Mistress Gray. We march within the hour.'

'Why?'

'Rupert is at Knaresborough, barely a day's march from York. We've no choice but to lift the siege and intercept him.'

'There'll be a battle?'

He nodded. 'Without doubt. We're facing a formidable foe, Perdita. It will be bloody.'

'What do you want of me?' Perdita swung her feet out of bed.

He had to look away and made a pretence of packing his box. Rupert of the Rhine made a less formidable foe than a beautiful woman in a thin chemise. Her bare feet padded on the floor boards and cloth rustled as she dressed.

'I want you back in Warwickshire,' he muttered and dared to turn around. She had her back to him, apparently lacing her stays over her petticoats. 'One thing for certes, you can't stay here. Once the siege is lifted, this village will be prey to the inhabitants of the city. I can send you south to Selby or...'

'Or I can come with you,' Perdita turned and looked over her shoulder. 'You know I have some skill with the wounded and I could be useful.'

'You would also be in the most incredible danger.' Adam ran a weary hand across his forehead. 'Should we not prevail...'

She held up a knife, the early morning light glinting on its honed blade. 'Ludovic gave me this. My honour will not be lost without a fight.'

Adam looked at the little weapon. If the baggage train were attacked, it would be useless but if it gave her confidence then he was in no position to argue.

He remembered a conversation he had with young Ashley on their way to Fairfax. 'I have a thought that will keep you where you are safe and your dubious skill with a knife should not need to be put to a test. Pack your things and find something to eat. We leave at daybreak.'

She took a step toward him, her fingers touching the chain of the locket he wore around his neck.

'You still have it.'

His hand closed over her fingers. 'I wear it always. It is my charm.'

Her lips curved uncertainly. 'Poor protection against a sword or a well-aimed musket.' She pulled away from him and handed him the heavy buff leather coat. He shrugged it on and stood quite still as she laced it. When he reached for his back and breast plate she was there before him, strapping on the armour like a good squire. He stood still as she tied the yellow silk sash around it and handed him his sword and baldrick.

Perdita gestured at his box. 'I'll see to your belongings,' she said, her eagerness to not seem to be a burden to him palpable.

He allowed himself a smile. 'Thank you. As I see you are determined to be a model camp follower, meet me downstairs.'

He sought out young Ashley and the young man readily agreed to Adam's suggestion.

'I'll see her safely bestowed,' he said.

Adam swung himself into the saddle as Perdita came out of the inn. He gestured for her to join him and introduced Richard Ashley.

'Richard's home is at Barton only a few miles from where we'll meet Rupert. He'll take you there. You will be as safe there as anywhere.' He jerked his head at Richard. 'I'll leave you in Richard's capable hands.'

She stood at his knee and put her hand on his bridle. 'God keep you safe, Adam.'

Impulsively he bent and kissed her forehead, her skin cool and dry beneath his lips. He dared not think about what the next few days would bring, or allow himself for even a moment in time to dare to dream.

He jerked back upright in the saddle. 'And you, Perdita. I shall see you when this matter is settled.' He wheeled his horse. 'Watch over her, Ashley.'

'Of course, sir. She'll be safe at Barton. Thank you, sir.'

Richard Ashley regarded Perdita's sturdy pony with a bemused smile.

'This nag has four legs, but that's about the best that can be said of him,' he said as he hoisted her into the saddle.

'You need not thank Adam Coulter for playing nursemaid to me, Captain,' Perdita said as they started off.

He smiled at her. 'You mistake me, Mistress Coulter. While it is a great pleasure to have your company, it means I have a few precious hours with my wife and son and for that I am exceeding grateful.'

She looked at his gentle face. He could surely not be much older than Robin Marchant. A young man who should have been at home with his wife watching his son grow, not escorting her through a countryside torn by war.

'You don't have the look of a soldier about you, Captain,' she remarked.

He shook his head. 'If the truth be told, I only took up arms to support my father. It's been a hard couple of years and I fervently pray that this coming battle will decide the matter.'

'And then will you return home?'

He shook his head. 'I doubt it. I'm honour bound to see this thing through.'

'You sound like my kinsman,' Perdita said. 'Only he wore the king's colours.'

And died for them.

Richard Ashley nodded. 'Men of honour carry the colours of both sides, Mistress Coulter.'

Men of honour, she thought. What did that mean? Robin, Simon, Denzil, even Adam had talked of honour, but where was the honour in Englishmen killing Englishmen, brother facing brother across the battlefield.

But yet they weren't brothers, Denzil and Robin and Adam. Cousins, nothing more. Denzil and Robin didn't know Joan's secret. To them Adam was still their bastard half-brother and she wondered if they were with Rupert marching toward the gates of York.

Ashley's home at Barton Grange was a low, grey stone manor house which stood to one side of the village. Roses entwined around the doorway and it exuded a sense of peace and tranquillity. Perdita looked quickly at her escort and saw the yearning on his face.

'Richard!'

A young woman, no more than a girl, had come running from the house, her skirts in her hand, her hair loosed from the cap she carried in the other hand. He slid off his horse, scooping her into his arms.

'Kate! Oh, Kate, it is good to see you.'

Oblivious to Perdita and the servants who gathered at the stable door and windows, the young couple kissed. A boy came forward and took the reins of the horses. He held out his hand and Perdita slid off her mount. She straightened her skirts and waited patiently until Richard and his young wife remembered propriety and drew apart.

The girl blushed, hastily rearranging her disordered dark honey-blonde hair back beneath the cap as she dropped Perdita a curtsey.

'Kate, this is my friend Major Coulter's wife.'

The two women exchanged courtesies and Kate waved her guest toward the house.

'Please come inside.' Kate stood aside, slipping her arm into the crook of her husband's elbow. 'Richard, how long have you got?'

'A short time only, love,' he said. 'Where's young Tom?'

'Upstairs with Ellen.'

They entered the cool interior of the house. The long, low-ceilinged parlour smelt of fresh beeswax polish and roses from the bowl of freshly picked flowers that stood on the table.

'Please don't feel you must entertain me,' Perdita said with a smile. 'Make the most of your time together. I see you have some books on that shelf. I shall be quite content.'

Kate hesitated. 'If you will not think me rude?'

Perdita shook her head and Kate Ashley smiled. Like her husband, she seemed impossibly young to be confronted with war.

'I will see you get some refreshment.' Kate looked up at her husband. 'Come and see Tom. He has grown so since you last saw him and is talking.'

Perdita smiled to herself as she followed their voices as they disappeared up the stairs. A servant set a tray down on the table with food and drink. Perdita selected a book and settled herself in the large oaken chair by the window overlooking the garden.

'Mistress Coulter?'

She had been so engrossed in the book she had not heard Richard Ashley. He stood at the door, spinning his hat in his hand.

'I regret I must leave now.'

She stood up. 'So soon? Thank you Captain Ashley. God go with you.'

'I will tell the major that you are safely bestowed.'

Perdita wondered what a good wife would be expected to say and said with a smile, 'And please assure him my prayers are with him.'

The young man inclined his head. 'Of course.' He bowed. 'Good day, mistress.'

Through the window she watched as Richard Ashley stooped from the saddle to kiss his young wife before turning his horse and riding out through the gates.

Kate turned back towards the house, and as she entered the parlour, the brave smile belied the tears that glinted in the afternoon light

'I apologise for neglecting you, Mistress Coulter.'

Perdita shook her head. 'Please, I bid my,' she paused, the lie once more coming to her lips, 'husband farewell this morning, there is no need to pretend an indifference to his departure you do not feel.'

Kate Ashley sank on to a chair and leaned her head on her hands.

'We seem to have had so little time together,' she said. 'We were wed but a year when the war came.' She looked up at Perdita. 'Have you been wed long?'

Perdita shook her head and changed the subject. 'You have a child?'

Kate brightened. 'Thomas. He was born not long before the

war began.' The shadows descended again. 'He has barely seen his father in all that time.'

'May I meet him?'

Kate's eyes brightened. 'Of course! He is upstairs with his nurse. Come and I will show you to the guest chamber and then we will visit Tom.'

Thomas Ashley was a dark-haired, slender child, who resembled neither parent. When Perdita remarked on this, Kate laughed.

'He is indeed a changeling. My father-in-law is of the opinion that he favours Richard's mother, but she is long dead and I have no likeness to compare. Do you have children, Mistress Coulter?'

Perdita hesitated. 'No... no.' The old pain caught at her voice.

Kate gave her a look of absolute understanding but before she could speak. Thomas, awkward in his skirts, toddled over to Perdita and held out a wooden horse.

'Horsey.'

Perdita took the toy and slipped down to her knees, her skirts billowing around her.

'See, Thomas,' she said trip-trapping the horse across the floor, 'the horse is going to visit his friends.'

The horse's friends were to be found in a wooden Noah's ark. Playing with the child made it possible for both women to forget for a couple of hours, the terrible danger that the men they loved would face in the morning.

Chapter Thirteen

MARSTON MOOR, 2 JULY 1644

'H e's not coming?' Hewitson muttered dourly as Adam rode up beside him, fresh from a hasty conference behind the lines. 'Ye're going to tell me that Rupert's decided not to give battle. Why else is't infantry moving?'

'The Generals are deploying most of the foot towards Tadcaster. They think Rupert means to break south,' Adam replied.

'Oh aye? Mayhap the generals have got it wrong.' Hewitson pointed across the moor. 'See yonder, that body of horse?'

Adam nodded.

'Rupert's men. They've been watching us for some time.'

As Hewitson indicated, the distant horsemen wheeled and turned away.

'So we know what t'generals think. What do you think?' Hewitson looked at his commander.

Adam still watched the place where the horsemen had been. 'I know Rupert. I believe he intends to force a fight and settle the matter, if not today then tomorrow. Sweet Jesus.' Where the little group of horsemen had stood, now a much larger force gathered and more beside them until it seemed the entire sky line became one line of soldiery.

'Seems you were right, Coulter,' Hewitson noted. 'How are we expected to hold 't field? With t'infantry gone, we've but six thousand horse.'

Adam shook his head. 'We'll never hold that number, and if they should prevail then our foot are strung out between here and Tadcaster. Idiots!' He looked up at the sky. 'And it's going to rain again.'

'Looks like battle it is.' Hewitson sighed. ''Tis the waiting I hates the most.'

Adam nodded. 'Let's deploy the men along the slope a little further.'

A wry grin flashed across Hewitson's face. 'You're not going to fool them into thinking we've more men than we have?'

Adam shrugged. 'If nothing else it will give the men something to do. Oh, and tell them that the mark of the day is a white favour in the helm.'

As Hewitson wheeled his horse and trotted across to the troops, Adam pulled a kerchief from his jacket and tore a sizeable piece from it. He unbuckled his helmet and fixed the scrap of cloth to the crown. It seemed an insubstantial distinction between himself and the other Englishmen he faced across the field.

He narrowed his eyes and scanned the force facing him. Goring, he guessed from the colours. It was unlikely that the Marchants would be here today and for that he was thankful. Another heavy shower of rain scudded across the field and Adam hunched his shoulders. Despite the rain it was warm, and beneath his cuirass and buff leather coat he was damp with sweat.

'The general's compliments, Major, but could you move your troops forward fifty yards?'

Adam turned at the sound of young Richard Ashley's voice.

'My compliments to the general. It will be done,' he replied, quickly relaying the instructions to his sergeant. He turned back to the young man. 'I trust you found your wife well yesterday?'

'Indeed, sir. My little lad is talking now.'

'How old is he?'

'Three, sir.'

'And my wife?' If there was the slightest hesitation before the word 'wife' Richard Ashley did not notice.

'No doubt gossiping with mine, sir.' Ashley blushed slightly. 'Probably about us.'

'Quite likely,' Adam smiled, doubting very much that Perdita Gray would be sharing his bad habits with Kate Ashley. 'God willing, we shall see them both again before too much longer.'

Richard Ashley saluted and wheeled his horse, cantering back to Fairfax's position.

For some reason best known to the prince, the royalists did not take advantage of the disorder in the parliamentary lines, giving time for the infantry to return to the field intact.

The day wore on and by late afternoon both sides faced each other across Marston Moor in battle order. Despite some desultory cannon fire from the left flank, neither side moved and the hours dragged by. The parliament soldiers began to chant psalms. While it provided some relief from the boredom and a cincture to their taut nerves, Adam found it an eerie sound and in many ways more discomforting than the guns.

He rose in his stirrups and surveyed the field for the tenth time that afternoon. To his left stretched a colourful array of flags and pennants, weapons glinting in the late afternoon sun.

'I don't like this ground,' Adam muttered scanning the field before him. Fairfax's horse on the right wing certainly had the worst of the land.

While the bulk of the parliamentary force had been arrayed along a gentle slope, the moor between Sir Thomas's cavalry and the enemy was covered in furze. The only clear access lay along a narrow lane, running at right angles to their position, bounded on one side by a ditch and on the other by a hedge lined with royalist muskets.

It must have been past seven in the evening when Adam detected a general wavering in the royalist lines, as if they had decided that no battle would be fought that day.

'They're surely not going to fight now,' Hewitson grumbled, shifting in his saddle. 'It'll be dark in a couple of hours.'

Adam agreed. To distract himself from his hunger, he turned his mind away from the thought of battle and turned instead to the problem of Perdita and how he could contrive to return her safely to Preswood. His gloved hand rose to his breast where the silver locket lay heavy against his skin.

A mighty cry from the left flank roused him from his reverie. The parliamentary horse, commanded by an Eastern Association man by the name of Cromwell, charged, taking some of the infantry with them.

Facing Cromwell, Prince Rupert's unbeatable cavalry, for once not the first to charge, fell back. The great guns from both sides began to flash and roar and the field quickly become hazy with smoke.

Adam's heart raced and his guts tightened as the order for Fairfax's cavalry to charge came too late for surprise. Fairfax, as always heedless of his own safety, took the head of his troops. Adam, as part of Fairfax's life guard, followed close behind.

Goring just had to wait and cut the Parliamentary horse to pieces as it picked its way through the furze and the hazards of the lane and the massive ditch that stood in their path.

To Adam's relief, most of his men got across safely and they could regroup in time to launch a hasty charge on Goring's line. The first impact of the assault caused the royalist line to waver and break. Sword on sword, the parliamentarians pushed Goring's men until some turned to flee with Fairfax's men hard at their heels.

Adam reined in beside his commander. Blood poured down the general's face from a slash to his right cheek, but Fairfax, breathless and exultant, did not appear to have noticed.

'Sir, shall I try to rally the horse?'

Fairfax turned his gaze on Adam, his eyes bright. 'Damn it, Coulter. We can't hope to bring them back to the fight now. We need help from Cromwell.'

'Sir, your face.'

Fairfax put his hand up to his cheek and looked in amazement as the tips of his gloves came away bright with blood. 'Must have been a sword,' he mused. 'No matter. Coulter, rally your own men and see what can be done.'

Adam had precious few men left to rally. Some he had lost at the ditch, others were probably halfway to York. Those few he could find, he summoned once more to Fairfax's colours and they plunged back into the smoke filled, rain-sodden slaughterhouse. Fairfax himself had been swallowed up in the fray.

Those of Goring's horse that had stayed on the field had charged straight through the parliamentarian lines and were no doubt indulging themselves in the baggage train, but the innocents among the baggage would have to fend for themselves. For a moment Adam thought of Perdita and sent a silent prayer of thanks that she had not come with him. He turned his weary troopers toward the centre of the field where the royalist foot were putting up a last valiant stand.

It was not even dark when the last shots were fired on Marston Moor. Adam was to learn later that Fairfax, finding himself surrounded by enemy, had torn off the white favour in his helmet and crept behind the battle lines to find Cromwell on the left flank. Alerted to the problems on the right flank, the dour fens man had brought his cavalry up behind Goring, forcing him to turn and face him. Goring's men broke and fled. Save for a few stubborn pockets of resistance, the worst was over as dark finally claimed the moor and a bright, full moon cast its light on the slaughter.

Late in the evening, a violent thunderstorm broke over Barton. Kate Ashley looked up at the first crack. The mending she had been working on fell from her shaking hands to the floor as she glanced at the window.

'Was that gunshot?' she asked, her grey eyes wide with fear.

Perdita shook her head. 'No. Just thunder. Edgehill was fought but a few miles distant from my home. I will never forget the sound of the guns.'

Kate stood up and paced the floor, her hands twisting in her skirts.

'I can't take this uncertainty,' she said. 'How can you be so calm?'

Perdita's exterior of quiet patience came from years of practice, but within her breast her heart beat a rapid tattoo as she heard another sound that she knew was not thunder.

She rose to her feet and went to the window. Foolishness she knew for there would be nothing to see.

'That's not thunder.' Kate joined her.

'Mistress Ashley, we may see wounded at the door before this night is out. Is there anywhere warm and dry that they can be put?'

Kate turned uncomprehending eyes on her guest.

'Wounded?'

'They came after Edgehill. We will need bandages and water. What salves do you have in your stillroom?'

Kate nodded. 'The barn is large enough and warm. I have no

experience of these things. Ellen, my maid, she keeps my stillroom. She knows what we will need. I'll fetch her.'

The guns fell silent at nightfall, leaving only the noise of the pounding rain. As Perdita had predicted, the first of the wounded trickled into the village of Barton and came to the door of the manor house. A surgeon came with them, a rough man who lacked half the skill of Ludovic, Perdita thought, but he did what little was within his powers and they were thankful to have him as the barn filled with the injured and maimed.

'Is it over?' Kate asked the young parliamentary soldier whose arm she bound.

'Ay Mistress. 'Tis a great victory for us.'

Kate clutched Perdita's arm. 'Perdita did you hear? 'Tis Parliament that has prevailed! God be praised.'

'Amen,' agreed Perdita with heartfelt thanks.

That seemed to be an invitation to those present to offer fervent prayers of thanksgiving for their deliverance from the foul fiend, Rupert.

'Where do they get this belief that he is the devil?' Perdita muttered half to herself.

Kate looked up. 'Rupert?'

'He's an extraordinary young man but quite human.'

'You know him?'

'I met him once,' Perdita admitted.

Kate looked at her and probably would have enquired further but another wave of wounded demanded her attention.

Shortly after dawn, Perdita stepped out into the yard, breathing the cold, damp morning air, thankful that the rain had stopped. She leaned against the old, stone walls of the house, letting exhaustion wash over her, trying to turn her mind from the hideous sights within the barn.

A man leading a horse and cart came down the lane from the

direction of Long Marston and Perdita straightened. It could only mean more wounded to be housed and cared for.

As he turned through the gates, she went to meet him, noticing that the latest comer was a well-dressed man of late middle age, his grey hair bared, his face white with exhaustion. Curiously he wore a gorget around his neck, the mark of an officer.

Perdita heard a gasp and turned to see Kate standing in the doorway, wiping her hands on her apron.

"Tis Richard's father, David Ashley,' she said.

Instinctively, Perdita caught the woman's arm but Kate shook her off, running toward the man with cart. He did not increase his pace but walked toward her, as if every step carried the weight of the world.

As she reached him, he dropped the reins of the horse and caught her.

'Kate, lass...'

Her eyes were wild as she struggled to break free. 'Richard! Dear God, Richard.'

'He can't hear you, lass.'

Kate broke his grip and ran around the cart. She stood staring wide eyed at the man who lay on the blood-soaked straw.

Her hand flew to her mouth and her father-in-law caught her as she staggered. She stood rigid in his grasp, staring transfixed at her husband as Perdita and Ellen ran to her side.

The man lying in the back of the cart was barely recognisable as Richard Ashley. His face was a bloodied mask, a rough blanket, soaked with blood, covered his torso and legs—and worse. Even from where she stood, Perdita could smell the unmistakable stench of a wound to the guts.

'He's not dead.' David Ashley said and his face twisted in anguish. 'I would to God he was, but he's not. When I found him this morning, I vowed I would bring him home. Perhaps that was foolishness.'

Perdita shook her head. 'No, you did the right thing. We'll care for him.'

Ashley blinked as if only seeing her for the first time. 'Who are you?'

'Perdita Gr... Coulter. I am Major Adam Coulter's wife. Can you have him carried inside?'

Ashley nodded and hailed two able-bodied soldiers sitting beside the barn. 'You two, carry my son indoors.'

The soldiers, recognising the poignancy of their task, lifted the wounded man gently and between them they carried him into the house and upstairs to a bed chamber.

Kate, restrained by her father-in-law, wept in his arms.

Perdita, following the men upstairs, caught sight of Tom in his nightshirt hiding in the shadows, clutching a wooden horse to his chest. She caught him in her arms and bundled him into the nursery with a white-faced maid.

'It's no place for a child,' she said. 'Keep him safe.'

A servant was despatched to fetch Kate's sister who lived nearby, and she came hurrying within the hour, a sensible woman, some ten years older than her sister. She and the maid, Ellen, excluded Kate from the bedchamber while the surgeon did what little he could.

Kate sat in her pleasant parlour, white-faced and silent, too shocked to weep. Perdita stayed with her, seeing herself in the younger woman and knowing words were no balm to her tortured soul.

The surgeon, bloodstained and reeking, stomped heavily down the stairs. He stood in the doorway and shook his head.

'There's nought I can do for him. If I were you, Mistress, I'd pray for a swift death.'

'No! No!' Kate wept into her sister's shoulder. 'Dear God, tell me this is some terrible nightmare.'

Ashley had replaced the surgeon in the doorway.

'Oh, lass.'

She pulled away from her sister and turned to face her father-in-law. 'This is your doing, David Ashley. He had no heart for this war. He only went out of respect for you.'

Ashley opened his mouth to say something and closed it again. 'There's nought I can say that will change the situation. Go to him, Kate. Stay with him.'

Without another word, she pushed past him and David Ashley subsided on to a chair at the table. He picked up a fallen petal from the rose bowl and turned the blood-red petal over in his fingers. It seemed like a long time before he looked up and his eyes caught Perdita's, registering her presence for the first time.

'Who did you say you were, Mistress?'

'I'm Adam Coulter's wife,' she said. 'Your son brought me here at my husband's request.'

He nodded slowly. 'Oh yes. Adam Coulter. Good man. He said he'd left a companion with Kate.'

'I'm sorry about your son.' The words seemed inadequate to the enormity of the situation.

'She's right.' David Ashley's fingers closed around the rose petal, crushing it. 'Richard had no heart for the fight. He should have remained here with Kate, where he rightly belonged.'

'I've lost someone like Richard,' Perdita said quietly. 'A good man who should have stayed quietly by his own hearth side.'

The man looked up, a frown creasing his forehead. 'Who?'

She shook her head. 'My kinsman.' She leaned forward. 'Tell me, sir, have you any news of my husband?'

He ran a hand across his eyes and shook his head. 'They had a hard time of it. Sir Thomas' men were cut to pieces. Richard fell in the first charge.'

Perdita closed her eyes, her breath coming in a sharp indrawn breath as she braced for the worst possible news.

David Ashley frowned. 'But Adam Coulter was alive and well

when last I saw him which was barely three hours ago. He came through and he's with his men, what's left of them. They've gone on to York.'

Perdita breathed again, relief flooding her. 'Praise the Lord,' she whispered.

It seemed wrong to show exultation in a place where death and grief were so overwhelming. She stood up and placed a hand on Ashley's shoulder.

'Colonel Ashley, you are plainly exhausted. Can I fetch you some food or drink?'

He nodded and Perdita went in search of the kitchen. When she returned ten minutes later, she found him asleep, his head resting on his arms. She laid the tray down beside him and made her way upstairs to her own bedchamber, intending to snatch a few hours of sleep herself.

The door to the chamber where Richard Ashley lay stood ajar, and Perdita steeled herself to enter the room of the dying man. Kate's sister sat beside the window looking down into the courtyard. She looked around at Perdita's entrance and shook her head.

Kate sat beside the bed, stiffly upright in a chair as if braced for some sort of action. Perdita looked down at what remained of the gentle young man who had brought her to this house. The blood had been cleaned from his face and the terrible wounds concealed by clean white bandages. A small fire had been lit in the fireplace to burn lavender, but the sweet, soothing scent could not mask the smell of impending death and it would not be a swift death. Perdita had seen enough wounds now to know that Richard Ashley may yet live several days.

'Ellen says he had over thirty wounds.' Kate spoke at last without moving or looking up at Perdita. 'How could men do that to another man, another Englishman?'

Perdita laid a hand on the other woman's shoulder. Kate reached up and grasped her hand. 'Will you pray with me, Perdita?'

Richard Ashley lay on the edge of death for three long days. His young wife barely left his side and his father sat in the parlour, a bottle of wine by his side, staring into an empty fireplace, his face a grey mask of exhaustion and grief. Kate's sister took young Thomas away to her own home, a mile distant, to be with her brood, returning to sit with her sister. Marooned in the grief-stricken house, Perdita found Kate's stoic silence almost too painful to bear as she recalled the last hours of Simon's life with a frightening clarity, and with no word from Adam, busied herself with the wounded in the barn, providing some relief for Kate from her bedside vigil.

Death came as a mercy and the Ashleys laid Richard to rest beside his mother in the little churchyard in the village. The family returned to the house and Kate, surrendering now to her grief and spent from weeping, had been put to bed with a sleeping draught. Her sister returned to Barton Hall and Perdita busied herself with the household responsibilities that Kate had abrogated.

'Mistress Coulter?'

Perdita looked up from the mending to see David Ashley, stooped and aged with grief, standing in the doorway to the parlour.

'I've had word that York has been taken and I have orders to return to my duties,' he said. 'I intend to take those wounded who can be moved. Do you also wish to come with me to find your husband?'

Perdita set her needlework aside and stood up, hoping she did not sound too eager as she said, 'Please, Colonel Ashley. I would be so grateful.'

He nodded. 'York is something over half a day's ride. It will be slower with the wounded. Do you have a horse?'

A brief smile flitted across Perdita's face as she recalled Richard Ashley's unfavourable view of her pony. 'Of sorts. Your son was less than complimentary about him.'

He nodded. 'Good. I'll tell Dickon to ready him. We will leave in the morning.'

Before she left, Perdita sought out Kate. The young widow, pale-faced, her eyes red-rimmed, sat in a chair by the window of her bedchamber. She barely looked up as Perdita entered.

'Kate?' Perdita said. 'I must leave today. I go with your father-in-law to York.'

Kate nodded. 'I have been remiss. Have you news of your husband?'

'Colonel Ashley tells me that he survived the battle and I hope... I pray... I will find him in York.'

Kate took her hand. 'I will pray that you do.'

Perdita's hand tightened on Kate's. 'I lost someone I love,' she said. 'The pain will ease and you may be blessed with a second chance.'

Kate released Perdita's hand and rose to her feet. She stood for a long moment, her arms wrapped around herself as she looked out into the garden, bright with the summer roses. She shook her head. 'No, Perdita. I think in this life we only have one chance at finding a true soul mate. I will never find another.'

Not given to impulse, Perdita threw her arms around the other woman and hugged her tight.

'None of us know what the future will bring. God grant he will keep you and your son safe and bring you some happiness in the future.'

Kate turned to face her, and for the first time in days a small smile lifted the girl's wan features. 'And you, Perdita. Treasure your time with your husband. Now go, David hates to be kept waiting.'

Chapter Fourteen

YORK, 17 JULY 1644

York had the look of a town that had endured a long siege. The walls and many of the buildings showed signs of damage by the great siege cannons Perdita passed on the way into the city, and the inhabitants, starved and wasted by disease, moved slowly through streets with boarded-up shops and homes.

Perdita accompanied Ashley to a building apparently designated for the care of the wounded. They had brought with them two wagonloads of men, mercifully the last of the wounded at Barton, and Perdita oversaw their disposition within the dark, fetid building, promising to return to see to them.

'I've made enquiries. They tell me your husband is lodged at the White Hart.' David Ashley's shadow fell across her as she saw to the bandages of one of the men she had nursed over the past week.

She stood and straightened her skirts. 'Thank you, Colonel.'

'Perhaps it is I who should thank you. Your presence at Barton was God sent.' He paused, his recent pain written raw in his eyes. 'It's Kate and young Tom I grieve for now. That I cannot be there to support them when they need me.' He inclined his head. 'Good day to you, mistress.'

Perdita gathered her small bundle of belongings and pushed her way through the crowded streets and the gathering dusk to the White Hart. The landlord indicated the room Major Coulter had appropriated, and gathering her skirts, Perdita climbed the stairs.

She knocked at the door, but as there was no reply she tried the latch and finding it unlocked, pushed open the door. Gauntlets, hat, boots, jacket, belt, breeches and shirt were strewn in a trail from the door to the bed, where Adam lay face down under the coverlet, his head buried in his arms. Perdita closed the door and tiptoed across to the bed. She laid a hand on his bare shoulder but he didn't stir and she had no wish to wake him. From his unshaven chin, she guessed that he had probably had precious little sleep since the battle. A dirty, bloodstained bandage circled his left forearm but otherwise he looked to have come through the battle without major injury.

She let out a soft sigh of relief and bent and kissed his bare shoulder, his skin salty beneath her lips.

She left him to slumber and took a simple meal in the parlour. She had considered asking the landlord for a separate room but it became obvious that the inn was fully occupied and it would have been strange for a wife to not wish to be with her husband, so she returned to Adam's chamber.

He had not moved.

She set the candle down on the table, picked up the battle stained clothing, folding them neatly on a chest. Looking around the room she saw nowhere else she could make up a bed, and having no desire to sleep on the floor, she bit her lip and considered the bed. It seemed perfectly adequate for two people to sleep in without unduly disturbing each other.

Stripping down to her chemise, she blew out the candle and slipped into bed beside him. She turned on her side and looked at his face on the bolster beside her, illuminated by the moonlight. She breathed in the mingled scents of sweat, horse and gunpowder and reaching out a tentative hand, she stroked the dark hair away from his forehead.

He moaned in his sleep and rolled over with his back to her. She longed to take him in her arms but with a deep shuddering breath, she turned over, curling herself up on the farthest side of the bed.

It was long past daylight before Adam awoke. He lay on his side with one arm flung across the hip of a young woman who slept with her back to him, curled into his embrace as if she belonged there. A cascade of dark-brown hair streamed across the bolster, tickling his nose.

He frowned and tentatively ran his hand the length of her slender body. He had a vague memory of stumbling back to his room, so bone weary he could scarcely put one foot in front of the other. Where had this nymph in his bed come from?

He propped himself up on one elbow and smiled as he pushed back a tendril of dark hair from her forehead and looked down into Perdita's sleeping face.

A wave of relief washed over him. She was safe. There was a rightness to her being not only safe but in his bed. He bent and kissed her forehead.

He closed his eyes and breathed in the sweet scent of her. He could no longer go on pretending the attraction between them did not exist. He wanted her here, beside him. He wanted desperately to fall into her arms at the end of the day. He wanted to love — and be loved by this woman.

She stirred and opened her eyes, rolling on to her back to look up at him. She smiled sleepily and a part of his anatomy responded to that thought and he realised that beneath the bed covers he was naked. This was surely a situation that would not end well.

'You're a heavy sleeper,' he said, drawing away from her.

Realisation flashed into her eyes and she scrambled upright, clutching the bedclothes to her. 'I'm sorry. I didn't mean to...' The colour rose to her cheeks. 'I thought I would sleep on the far side of the bed and you wouldn't even know I was there... I must have rolled.'

Adam smiled as the colour rose in her cheeks. 'I must have been dead to the world. God knows, I've had precious little sleep in the last weeks.'

Even the twelve hours he had just enjoyed was a poor compensation for the days with no more than a couple of hours sleep snatched in the corners of fields, even on horseback.

He put a hand to her face, cupping her cheek, noting the dirt of the battlefield still grimed under his nails. She leaned into his hand, her gaze holding his.

'Perdita,' he whispered hoarsely. 'We can't go on like this. The pretence has to end.'

Her breast rose and fell as she expelled a heavy sigh. 'The pretence we are married, or...'

He traced the line of her neck with his thumb, her skin soft against his calluses.

'Or the pretence that we are indifferent to each other, because I can't lie any more, not to myself and not to you,' he said.

Perdita raised her hand, laying it over his, her throat working as she said, 'Adam, is there hope for us?'

He frowned. 'Hope?'

'I sometimes think we are like feathers in the wind, tossed this way and that without any sense that we can control our destinies.'

'Is that why you agreed to marry Simon?'

She looked away, her hand dropping from his. 'He was something solid I could cling to, but his death has set me adrift again.' Her lips parted as she looked up at him. 'The wind blew me north to be with you. There must be a reason.'

He smiled. 'Am I solid enough for you?'

She shook her head. 'No. You are a soldier fighting a brutal war. I have seen too much death in the past days to have any hope of finding sanctuary in your arms, but,' she paused, her chest rose but did not fall, as she breathed out the words, 'but I am willing to take what shelter you can offer me. I... I love you, Adam Coulter.'

He closed his eyes. He had no words to answer her. Let his actions be his answer.

With both hands, he held her face, drawing her close until their noses brushed and he lowered his lips to hers. She answered his passion with a breathless intensity, their bodies melding as his hands slid down her neck, pushing the thin fabric of her chemise away from her shoulders. She breathed out, leaning in toward him, but as his fingers brushed the curve of her breasts, she pulled back, jerking his hands away.

'No! I can't.' She looked away, her face concealed behind a curtain of hair.

Adam fought to control his own ragged breathing and turned her face back to look at him, appalled by the tears that brimmed from her eyes.

'Perdita, I'm sorry.'

She shook her head. 'It's not you, Adam. God alone knows how I want nothing more than to be with you, but...' she swallowed. 'Samuel Gray.' The tears overflowed, tracking unchecked down her cheek and he understood. The man who had been her husband and shown her no tenderness, only brutality, now rose like a shadow between them.

'I am not Samuel Gray,' he said enunciating each word with care.

She touched his cheek and smiled. 'No, you're not, but I need time. I need to learn how love should be.'

For a very long moment neither spoke nor moved. Adam sighed and took the hand that she had reached out to him, turning it over in his own and kissing the palm, the soft mound of her thumb, the inside of her wrist.

'You are not a plaything that I will use and discard. When we make love, I will show you what it is to be with a man who loves you. I will make this right,' he said.

She blinked, scattering tears like raindrops on her cheeks. 'How?'

'To this world, you are my wife in name, I would have you my wife by right. If you would have me?' His hand closed over hers.

She dashed away the tears with her free hand. 'You would wed me?'

'I don't want you for a mistress, Perdita.' He could hear the impatience in his own voice. 'But I have nothing to offer you. I could be dead tomorrow. I realise I am a poor offering. Will you take me?'

Her brown eyes brimmed again but this time, a smile curled the corners of her mouth. 'Can we do it? Dare we? I don't care about tomorrow, Adam.'

Adam considered for a long moment. More to the point, how were they to regularise the matter, without the entire army of the north knowing they had been pretending to be man and wife these last weeks.

His mind cast around the town of York. Surely there must be a priest somewhere in this town who could, with the right persuasion, utter the words without the formalities of banns.

He kissed her hand again and drew back. 'Then it shall be. My first task for the day will be to find a priest. What did you do with my clothes?'

Perdita waved a hand in the direction of a chair. 'Over there.'

'Thank you,' he grunted and slid from underneath the bedcoverings and padded naked across to the neatly folded pile of battle-soiled garments. When he glanced back, she was seemingly absorbed in a close scrutiny of the farthest corner of the room.

He smiled at her modesty. She must have seen him naked in those days after he had been wounded and the Lord alone knew how many naked men she had dealt with over the last few days.

'You're laughing at me,' she said.

He shook his head as he pulled on his breeches. 'No. I am not laughing at you. I am—'

A knock at the door caused them both to start.

'What is it?' Adam bellowed at the locked door.

'Major Coulter?' A hesitant voice came from the other side.

'Yes.'

'The general's compliments but he requests you attend him.'

'Now?'

'Immediately.'

Adam blew out a breath. 'Very well. I shall be there presently.'

They waited until the sound of the messenger's boots had faded away before glancing at each other.

'Do you have to go?' she asked.

'I do,' he grumbled as he hunted through his chest for a clean shirt.

Perdita slid out of bed and crossed to Adam.

'Let me dress that arm,' she said.

He looked down at the soiled bandage. 'Later. It doesn't bother me.' Or at least it hadn't until she mentioned it.

'How did you do it?'

'This? A musket ball tore my sleeve. It's only a graze.' His mouth tightened. 'I was one of the fortunate ones, Perdita. You should see the general. He has a slash down the left hand side of his face that will mark him for life.'

Perdita nodded. 'I have some idea. I saw Richard Ashley and the others that came to Barton.'

Adam straightened at the name. 'Richard? I heard he had been wounded.'

'He's dead. A horrible lingering death, Adam.'

Adam flinched, he knew only too well the terrible ways a man could die. 'What a waste,' he muttered.

Impulsively he folded her in his arms. She felt so right. He buried his face in her hair, drinking in the scent of her. Reluctantly he pulled away, searching for his jacket, the torn, stained sleeve marking the passage of the pistol ball.

Perdita's fingers played with the ragged edges of the tear, stiff with blood. 'That needs cleaning.'

Adam looked down at her. 'Now you are starting to sound like a wife.'

She took the gorget from his hand and buckled it around his neck.

'Is this what a good officer's wife does?' she asked.

He straightened his crumpled collar over the piece of metal and kissed her upturned face, trying unsuccessfully not to run an approving eye over the womanly shape revealed beneath the chemise she wore.

'Good, *godly*, officer's wives don't keep their husbands away from their commanding officer.'

He retrieved his baldrick and sword which hung on the back of the chair and turned to Perdita. Stooping, he kissed her gently. 'I will return as soon as I can and we will make our plans.'

She slipped her arms around his neck and kissed him again.

'I will order supper for us. Don't be long.'

'Coulter! You took your time.' Sir Thomas Fairfax looked up from his paperwork.

Breathless, Adam swept off his hat and came to attention. 'My apologies, sir. I was catching up with some sleep.'

Fairfax tightened his lips to stop a smile. He winced and put his hand to his face. The surgeon had stitched the hideous slash well but it would leave an ugly, disfiguring scar.

'Don't make me smile, Coulter. It hurts. You were enjoying a reunion with your wife, I believe.'

'Sir.' Adam felt the heat rising to his cheeks, partly at the lie and partly at the truth.

'Well, your reunion will be short lived. We're marching out on the morrow.'

Adam looked surprised. 'But, sir, we've only just taken York.'

'All the more reason to move on and clean off the other areas of opposition, Scarborough and Pontefract to begin with. I will need your men ready to march by sunrise tomorrow.'

Adam studied his commander's ruined face. 'Sir, my men are exhausted. Surely another day' He refrained from making the observation that, in his opinion, cavalry were not best employed in siege work and that the next few weeks could mean little useful work for his men.

Fairfax shook his head. 'Tomorrow, Coulter. We need to move fast.'

Adam took a breath. 'The reason my wife came north was to tell me that my mother has died, I would beg your indulgence for a few days leave to go and see to matters on my estates.'

Fairfax picked up his pen and tapped it on the table.

'How long do you want?'

Adam swallowed. He hadn't thought this through, it had only come to him as he knocked on the door.

'The estate is to the north, near Newcastle. Three weeks?'

'Very well. Hewitson is capable enough to manage in your

absence, but I want you to report back to me by the second week in August, is that clear?'

'Sir, thank you.'

Adam turned to go but Fairfax's voice stopped him. 'Coulter, I'm sorry about your mother.'

Adam turned back to face him. 'So am I, sir.'

Chapter Fifteen

STRICKLAND, NORTHUMBERLAND, JULY 1644

Adam leaned forward on the pommel of his saddle and looked down at the solid, grey walls of his inheritance.

He had no specific memory of this place, but the smell of the heather and the feel of the gentle summer breeze that lifted his collar drew out something lost deep within him. He wondered if he had been happy here or had he been truly abandoned, unloved and alone? What manner of woman had Ann Coulter been to take the responsibility of the child born of her cousin's shame? How different would his life have been if Lord Marchant had not ridden up this same road, all those long summer days ago?

Beside him Perdita's pony jerked its head up with a snort of impatience.

'This is Strickland Castle? I think the title 'castle' is a bit of a misnomer,' Perdita said.

Adam had to agree. Heavily fortified farm house seemed closer to the mark. It had probably been built back in the days when the border lands were wild, lawless places. Time had softened the grey stone and some newer additions provided some modicum of comfort that had not been intended in the original design. Not unlike Preswood, the buildings stood around three sides of an open courtyard. However, the signs of neglect were obvious in the sunken roof of one of the wings, boarded up windows and a now - dry moat, overgrown with holly and long grass.

It didn't matter, it was now his piece of earth.

After the initial shock of Joan's revelation, he had come to an acceptance of his new place in the world. Joan had been right when she had said her brother was as good a father as any. For all his black and white view of the world, his uncle had been a fair man and he had borne his sister's shame as his own.

As to the identity of his father, he doubted the answers lay here at Strickland, but his own natural curiosity would have liked to have known the answer to that question. Now there was no one living who could tell him.

'Someone is at home,' Perdita remarked, indicating the thin line of smoke curling from a single chimney toward the rear of the building.

No one came out to meet him so he dismounted and tethered his horse to a hawthorn bush. He crossed to the old gates that barred entrance to the courtyard and lifted the heavy knocker. When no one answered, he knocked again and eventually a door beyond the gate creaked open and the sound of wooden soles clacking on cobbles grew closer to the gate.

The small door in the massive gates opened and the face of an old woman peered out. She blinked up at him, with eyes milky with cataracts.

'My name is—'

'I ken who you are,' the woman said. 'I held you in my arms when you were a bairn. Adam Coulter they called you.'

The back of Adam's neck prickled and Perdita's hand on his arm tightened.

'Who are you?'

'Mab,' the crone replied. 'Ye'll not remember me. You were nowt but a small bairn when he came for ye, but I'd know ye for Coulter, e'en without the lawyer sending word to expect ye. Yer mother is dead?'

Adam nodded.

'Then ye best come in, my lord. For lord of these lands ye are now.'

Adam stepped through the gateway and paused for a moment to look up at the building that surrounded him. Up closer, the unmistakable air of neglect hung over the homestead, from the ivy-covered walls and crumbling stonework to the broken windows and sagging guttering.

'When did Mistress Coulter die?' He addressed Mab's back.

She turned to look at him. 'Ten year she's bin in the grave now. Mistress Joan put in a caretaker but he died in the springtime and there's bin no one to collect the rents or tend to the land since then.' She stopped at a heavy oak door and turned to look at him. 'Ye're a soldier? I heard tell of wars being fought in the land again.'

Adam nodded.

Mab sighed heavily. 'Well there'll be no thought of you returning here for some wee while then?'

Adam hesitated and glanced at Perdita. Any thoughts he might have had of installing Perdita here were beginning to fade.

Mab waved at the door. 'Well, come in, come in. The best I can offer ye is the kitchen. It's warm and dry, not like the rest of the house.'

She ushered them into a flagged kitchen where a fire burned in the hearth, making the room almost unbearably hot. Here, in her domain, Mab turned to face them.

'Who's this?' She jerked a clawed hand at Perdita.

'My...' Adam glanced at Perdita. He had been about to say 'wife' but that small detail still had to be dealt with. The paucity of good inns between here and York had kept them apart at night.

'Betrothed,' Perdita interposed.

Mab nodded as if she approved of what she saw. 'How long are ye staying?'

'Only a few days.'

Mab nodded. 'I'll send the boy to stable your horses and ye can take your time to look over the place, but ye'll not like what ye see.'

Perdita took his hand. 'You go,' she said. 'I'll see what can be done for supper.'

He nodded, appreciative of her tact.

He wandered the dusty and deserted corridors trying to find some other memories, but he saw only the cobwebs and smelt the musty smell of a building too long shut up.

To his surprise, he found Mab in a large bedchamber, stoking a fitful fire into life.

She rose to her feet on his entrance, brushing dust from her skirts.

'This ''ere was Mistress Coulter's room. It's the best I can offer ye. I've made up the bed and the lady I'll put in the room across the corridor. 'Tis small but dry.'

'Is there a priest in the village?'

Mab's eyebrows lifted. 'Aye, if ye've a mind to see him, I can send the boy for him.'

'I presume I own his living?'

'Ye do.'

Good, that meant there would be no argument about tedious formalities. They could be wed on the morrow.

Mab laid her hand on a dusty box that stood on the table. 'I've not touched Lady Ann's papers. The key's in yonder pot.' She indicated a clay pot of some antiquity that stood on the window ledge.

'Tell me,' Adam said. 'What manner of woman was Lady Ann?'

Mab's face softened. 'Oh, she were a fine lady, sir. As good and gentle as any you'd want to meet. Broke her heart when Lord

Marchant came to fetch you. She was never wed and had no bairn of her own to hold.'

A shiver ran down his spine and in that moment, Adam had the strange sensation of seeing a grey-haired woman standing beside the fireplace in this very room, her hand resting on a cane.

'She had a twisted back,' he said.

Mab nodded. 'Ye remember? Aye, a hunchback she was. There were never any lads to court her, except for what they saw in her lands. She chose not to marry. I'll leave you, sir, and send yer lady up to you.'

When Mab had gone, Adam opened the box. Within were deeds and various estate papers, and at the very bottom of the box he found a bundle of letters tied with string. His heart jumped as he recognised the writing as Joan's.

He sat down beside the now -blazing fire and pulled his boots off. He propped his feet on a stool and undid the ribbon that bound the packet of letters. The last letter turned out to be the first and was written by his uncle, the man he had always known as his father.

'*My dear cousin, it grieves me to be the bearer of sad tidings, but my beloved sister Joan is gravely ill and the doctors fear for her life. She cries piteously for her babe and I fear I have no choice but to fetch the child to Marchants. I have promised Joan that I will do this and more. I have given her my word on my honour that the child will be raised as a child of mine. My wife has protested most vigorously but I will prevail, for reasons best known to myself. Expect me within the month. Yr servant John M.*'

Adam stared at the letter, wondering why he had never seen the affection Lord Marchant had held for his sister. It had been masked by the antipathy, Sofia, Lady Marchant, had displayed to the bastard child. Maybe, he considered, his uncle's decision to bring Adam to Marchants had been the beginning of the long disintegration of the relationships in the Marchant family. He had always been the cuckoo in the nest. Now he understood why.

Adam turned to Joan's letters and read an account of her slow recovery and her joy at being reunited with her child.

'...*although I cannot claim him as my own, to see him daily and to hold him as a proper aunt. You ask how my brother prevailed on Lady Marchant to accept his tale and it is sad to relate that I suspect it is because it is common talk at court that Lady Sophia has taken a young lover to her bed. To avoid her own scandal she is willing to tolerate her husband's own infidelity, even though he is the most faithful of men.*'

Each letter had been written on the same date; Adam's birthday. Adam read the account of his life as he grew from skirts to a boy, schooled with his 'brother' Denzil, learning sword play and how to ride.

Robin's birth had brought great joy to the household, and then, within a few years, Lady Marchant's death, an event Adam remembered viewing with considerable relief. The letters ceased when Adam had gone to court, shortly before what would have been Ann Coulter's death.

As he read each letter he consigned it to the flames, watching as the edges caught and the ink momentarily darkened before the paper turned black and dissolved into the red heart of the fire.

As he consigned the final letter to the flames, watching as the last tie with his mother smouldered, exploded into flame and vanished, the door opened and Perdita entered followed by Mab, carrying a large tray with a steaming bowl of rabbit stew, fresh bread and a bottle of wine. He indicated the smaller table beside the fireplace and Mab left them alone to their supper.

Perdita looked up at the wall around the fireplace. She pointed past the rows of grim-faced ancestors of the last century to a small head and shoulders study of a dark haired child.

'Adam, have you seen that portrait?'

He rose to his feet and took it down from the wall. He recognised the style and the initials in the corner JM—Joan Marchant.

'Joan's work,' he said.

'You,' Perdita said.

'Me,' he echoed and turned to face her.

'Are you sorry you came?' she asked.

'No. I knew I never belonged at Marchants and now I understand why. The fact remains I will always bear the stain of being bastard-born but there's nothing I can do to change that and nothing here to give any indication as to who my father may have been.'

He looked around the room and hefted a heavy sigh. 'As for my inheritance, it's in worse repair then I thought. This is probably one of the few inhabitable rooms in the whole place.'

Perdita took a sip of her wine. 'When the war is over, Adam, we will make this a home. A place where we can be happy. A place for' she broke off and a shadow crossed her face. He wondered if she had been about to say 'for children'.

He smiled. 'Until then, we must seize our moments.' He took her by the hands and pulled her to his feet, so she stood facing him. 'Tomorrow, my dearest Perdita, we will find the priest and be wed, and for such time as we can we will pretend that the world beyond these walls does not exist. This moment is ours.'

She wound her arms around his neck, looking into his face, searching his eyes. He bent his head and their lips met, and he knew he could never let her go again. Like the feathers in the wind Perdita had talked about, they had caught each other and were now bound together. Whatever lay in their future, for now they were content.

THE END

If you enjoyed this book,
read on for an excerpt from

Acknowledgments

Thanks are owed, as always, to my wonderful writer friends in the Saturday Ladies Bridge Club, without whom my writing world would be very lonely.
And to my ever patient husband, DJB, who has to live with my imaginary friends.

About the Author

Mystery, history, romance and ghosts...

Award winning Australian author, Alison Stuart learned her passion for history from her father. She has been writing stories since her teenage years but it was not until 2007 that her first full length novel was published. A past president of the Romance Writers of Australia, Alison has now published eight full length historical romances and inumerable short stories have appeared in anthologies. Many of her stories have been shortlisted for international awards and BY THE SWORD won the 2008 EPIC Award for Best Historical Romance.

Alison has travelled extensively and lived in Africa and Singapore. Her soldier heroes may come from her varied career as a lawyer in the military and fire services. These days when she is not writing she is travelling and routinely drags her long suffering husband around battlefields, castles and more recently, derelict gold fields.

Connect with Alison at her website

www.alisonstuart.com

For all her latest news and to sign up to her newsletter for exclusive free reads, contests and more...

Alison Stuart

HER REBEL HEART

A romance of the English Civil War

Her Rebel Heart - Chapter One

Kinton Lacey Castle, Herefordshire
23 July, 1643

S tartled out of an uneasy doze by the crackle of musket fire, Deliverance sent books and papers flying as she rummaged through the detritus on the table in her search for the flint. As the candle sputtered into life, the door opened and her steward, Melchior Blakelocke, stood outlined in the doorway, holding a covered lantern.

"Are we being attacked?" Deliverance asked.

"I don't think so," Melchior replied. "In fact, my lady, I think it is our besiegers who are being attacked."

Hope sprang in Deliverance's heart. "Is it Father? Has he come to relieve us?"

She reached for the elegant French Wheelock musket her father used for hunting, running her hand over the well-polished wood of the stock. It had a kick that threatened to dislocate her shoulder every time she used it, but she took pride in her mastery of the weapon.

Outside, the entire garrison of Kinton Lacey Castle had deployed along the walls, but to her relief, the firing and shouts came from beyond the crumbling walls of the old castle. She took her now accustomed vantage point on the northern tower of the bastion gate and squinted into the darkness and confusion.

Smoke and flame from burning outbuildings lent a surreal light to the melee of men that whirled and danced in the shadows as if re-enacting some ancient pagan ceremony. Only the clash of steel instead of cymbals brought home the grim purpose of the bizarre pageant.

Two men on horseback appeared out of the smoke and cantered towards the castle. Backlit by the

fires, they could have been a pair of vengeful spirits.

Her heart pounding, Deliverance raised her musket and fired, cursing in a most unladylike manner as the musket ball skimmed past the two men, taking the taller man's hat. His horse, startled by its rider's jerk of alarm, reared up depositing the soldier on the ground. For a moment he lay still, before rising to his hands and knees. Shaking his head, he rose slowly to his feet, casting an upwards glance in the direction of the castle, as he dusted off his hat and remounted his horse.

Melchior cleared his throat. "While that is excellent shooting, I think you will find they are friends not foes."

Deliverance's stomach lurched. "How can you tell?"

"They wear the orange sash of the parliamentary forces, my lady."

Deliverance leaned the musket against the wall, clenching and unclenching her hand in an effort to disguise her shaking fingers. Nausea rose in her throat. It was the first time she had fired the weapon intending to kill and she had nearly killed one of their own relieving force.

She took a deep breath, struggling to regain her composure as the two men came to a halt at the bridge over the castle's defensive ditch. Facing them were the stout oaken gates to the castle that Deliverance had shut on her foe two weeks earlier.

"Hold your fire." The man she had shot at called up to the defenders. "We are sent by Sir John

Felton to relieve this castle."

Deliverance picked up her musket and drew back to a vantage point where she could see without being seen. "You answer, Melchior."

Melchior cast her a sidelong glance and stepped forward to the battlements. "Your name, sir?" "Captain Luke Collyer."

"How do we know they've come from Father?" Deliverance prompted her steward. "How do I know you are sent by his lord-ship?" Melchior demanded.

The man who had identified himself as Captain Luke Collyer produced a paper from his jacket and waved it at the wall.

"These are my orders. While I don't wish to appear churlish, sir, we have no great desire to remain outside these walls when those knaves could be back at any moment."

"What do you mean?" Melchior asked, leaning further over the ramparts.

"We appear to have seen off your besiegers for the moment." The man's voice rose to make himself

heard by all on the castle wall.

Deliverance drew a sharp intake of breath as relief flooded through her. The siege was over, but she still had to be careful. She put no trust in Farrington not to try and gull her in this fashion.

"Very well, Melchior, let them in, but I want every man with a weapon to have it trained on them." She tapped a fingernail on the stock of her musket. "I will meet them in the Great Hall."

"May I suggest a change of dress, madam?"

She looked down at her breeches. "Demure and ladylike?" Melchior nodded. "Demure and ladylike."

OTHER TITLES by Alison Stuart

Historical Romance

And Then Mine Enemy

Guardians of the Crown Series

By The Sword (Book 1)

The King's Man (Book 2)

Exile's Return (Book 3)

Paranormal Historical Romance

Gather The Bones

Secrets In Time